She Was  og.

That's just the way it was.

But now something was happening between him and Rachel. Something new, something different. Something threatening...

Rachel loved him. Or believed she did. It was the vulnerable, yearning way she was looking at him. It was the way her kisses started out playful and turned into something soft and dark real, real fast.

He was enjoying her treating him like a prince—he couldn't deny it. But when push came to shove, he was the same old frog.

For once in his life, though—for Rachel—he desperately wanted to be that prince she belicved in....

Dear Reader,

Welcome to Silhouette Desire—where you're guaranteed powerful, passionate and provocative love stories that feature rugged heroes and spirited heroines who experience the full emotional intensity of falling in love!

This October you'll love our new MAN OF THE MONTH title by Barbara Boswell, *Forever Flint.* Opposites attract when a city girl becomes the pregnant bride of a millionaire outdoorsman.

Be sure to "rope in" the next installment of the exciting Desire miniseries TEXAS CATTLEMAN'S CLUB with *Billionaire Bridegroom* by Peggy Moreland. When cattle baron Forrest Cunningham wants to wed childhood friend Becky Sullivan, she puts his love to an unexpected test.

The always-wonderful Jennifer Greene returns to Desire with her magical series HAPPILY EVER AFTER. *Kiss Your Prince Charming* is a modern fairy tale starring an unforgettable "frog prince." In a sexy battle-of-the-sexes tale, Lass Small offers you *The Catch of Texas.* Anne Eames continues her popular miniseries MONTANA MALONES with *The Unknown Malone.* And Sheri WhiteFeather makes her explosive Desire debut with *Warrior's Baby,* a story of surrogate motherhood with a twist.

Next month, you'll really feel the power of the passion when you see our new provocative cover design. Underneath our new covers, you will still find six exhilarating journeys into the seductive world of romance, with a guaranteed happy ending!

Enjoy!

Joan Marlow Golan
Senior Editor, Silhouette Desire

Please address questions and book requests to:
Silhouette Reader Service
U.S.: 3010 Walden Ave., P.O. Box 1325, Buffalo, NY 14269
Canadian: P.O. Box 609, Fort Erie, Ont. L2A 5X3

KISS YOUR
PRINCE CHARMING
JENNIFER GREENE

SILHOUETTE Desire®

Published by Silhouette Books

America's Publisher of Contemporary Romance

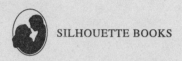

SILHOUETTE BOOKS

ISBN 0-373-76245-3

KISS YOUR PRINCE CHARMING

Copyright © 1999 by Jennifer Greene

This edition published by arrangement with Harlequin Books S.A.

® and TM are trademarks of Harlequin Books S.A., used under license. Trademarks indicated with ® are registered in the United States Patent and Trademark Office, the Canadian Trade Marks Office and in other countries.

Visit us at www.romance.net

Printed in U.S.A.

JENNIFER GREENE

lives near Lake Michigan with her husband and two children. Before writing full-time, she worked as a teacher and a personnel manager. Michigan State University honored her as an "outstanding woman graduate" for her work with women on campus.

Ms. Greene has written more than fifty category romances, for which she has won numerous awards, including three RITAs from the Romance Writers of America in the Best Short Contemporary Books category, and a Career Achievement Award from *Romantic Times Magazine*. She was also recently inducted into the Romance Writers of America Hall of Fame.

Dear Reader,

This is the second book in my HAPPILY EVER AFTER series. Do you remember *The Frog Prince* fairy tale? Where the girl has to kiss the frog to get the prince? Well, personally, I thought that story needed a drastic feminist update. In my version, there's a woman, of course. And a man who's a prince of a guy. But today's woman is way smarter than in generations past, yes? No way, no how, would we be willing to kiss any frogs....

Unless, of course, there was an extraordinarily good reason for doing so.

I hope you like the story! And wishing you all my best—

Jennifer Greene

One

Rachel Martin had *had* it. She zipped her ancient yellow VW into the driveway, cut the engine and then scowled at the debris piled on the passenger seat. There was no way she could carry the mail, groceries, her purse and her briefcase into the house in one haul—but she was too darn hot and cranky to make two trips.

Since the divorce, of course, Rachel had learned the obvious. A woman could always find a way to do the impossible. Sometimes the impossible was just a little more challenging than other times.

Once she climbed out of the car, she stuck the mail between her teeth, hooked the key ring on a finger and then used both arms to scoop up the grocery sack, briefcase, and purse tote. The success of her hauling mission seemed assured until she tried slamming the car door closed with her fanny—which jostled everything, particularly threatening to topple the ice cream at the top of the overstuffed grocery bag.

Oh, man. She needed that ice cream. She deserved it. The whole day had been a nonstop test of sanity. The air-conditioning had malfunctioned at work. All six of her engineers had been testy and demanding. She'd skipped lunch and then had to work late. Her blue linen suit had more limp wrinkles than a shar-pei's face, her right stocking had a run and her stomach was making pitiful growling sounds of starvation. The unrelenting heat was so unfair. This was Milwaukee, for Pete's sake. Cool nights should have been a guarantee by the middle of September—particularly by seven o'clock—and yet the temperature still registered a mean, cruel ninety degrees with enough humidity to melt steel.

Carefully juggling her packages, sweat drooling down the back of her neck, Rachel mentally pictured her life ten minutes from now. Forget chores. Forget the sounds of lawn mowers and honking cars and kids shrieking as they skateboarded down the sidewalks of the old neighborhood. She could be inside her rented house in two minutes. Naked in six. A few seconds after that, she could be draped under the air-conditioning vent in her living room, dipping a spoon into an entire gallon of Fudge Ripple, with an old classic Spencer Tracy/Katharine Hepburn flick plugged into the VCR.

The fantasy was almost as satisfying as sex. Maybe even better. Sex wasn't a remote possibility in her life right now, where ice cream was definitely a can-do.

"Ms. Martin? Wait, Ms. Martin!"

She recognized Leo Rembrowsky's voice coming up behind her, and any other time she wouldn't have minded chatting a few minutes with her elderly neighbor. Leo was okay. Occasionally he'd tried to peek in her bathroom window and he was an incurable busybody, but mostly he was just lonely since his wife died. Swiftly she turned around, so Leo could see her arms were completely stuffed and she was in no position to stop and visit—yet he didn't seem to notice.

"I been waiting for you." He huffed and puffed up the driveway until he caught up with her, his Slavic accent even heavier than usual. "You're late today. I wait outside in the heat. But I thought you should know. Mr. Stoner was in big car accident."

Her heart clutched. She dropped her briefcase and yanked the mail out of her mouth. "You mean Greg? *Our* Mr. Stoner?"

"Yes, yes. I heard from Tilda. She heard on scanner. Then Josie, she call the hospital—"

Vaguely Rachel heard the details of the neighborhood gossip vine. Vaguely she was aware of the bloodred sun, dropping fast now, painting the maple leaves gold and brushing the sky with dusky sunset shadows. Life just seemed so everyday normal that it took a jolting few seconds for Rachel to believe something had really happened to Greg. "Mr. Rembrowsky, which hospital? And do you know how badly he was hurt?"

Leo crouched down to pick up the spray of envelopes. "St. John's, I hear. It was three-car pileup. Early afternoon. Tilda called hospital, but no one would say how he is. You have to be family or nobody wants to talk to you. But I still thought you would want to know."

"I do. I did. Thank you, Mr. Rembrowsky, and I'm so sorry you waited out in the heat...."

He straightened up and piled the mail on top of her grocery sack. "You just tell me when you find out news, okeydoke? And if there's something we neighbors can do, you say."

"Okeydoke. I promise." She hustled up the sidewalk, shifted everything so she could unlock the back door, then swiftly jogged in and dropped all the debris on the counter in her yellow-and-white kitchen.

Inside, the air conditioner was wheezing and gasping like a four-pack-a-day smoker, but at least it was working—for now. Like most homes in the neighborhood, her two-story frame house dated somewhere around the turn of the century. On the plus side, the rooms had personality and character and unique little architectural features. On the minus side, every appliance in the place had a capricious personality. Greg's theory was that she needed to get tougher and show the appliances who was boss.

Again her heart squeezed tight at the thought of Greg injured, and she quickly grabbed the phone book and searched for the hospital's number. Once she dialed and was stuck waiting for someone to answer, her gaze peered outside.

Her kitchen window overlooked his kitchen window. The distance between houses was a mere fifty yards, but the economic chasm between them might as well have been miles. Her rental house mimicked most structures in the respectable-turned-shabby neighborhood. Greg's elegant Victorian house, though, was the exception, and stood out like a treasured castle with its manicured lawn and wrought-iron balconies and gleaming casement windows. Why he lived alone in the big old white elephant, Rachel hadn't yet figured out—but over the last couple years, she'd spent countless hours in that house. They'd had dinner in his kitchen two nights ago. Cripes, she'd shared a cup of coffee with him just that morning.

Finally someone at the hospital answered. "Hello, this is Rachel Martin. I'm inquiring about a patient—Greg

Stoner—I believe he was brought in this afternoon after a car accident…'' Swiftly she crossed her fingers. "Oh, yes, of course I'm a relative. That's exactly why I'm asking—I just heard about the accident, and I'm his sister—"

The lie slipped out smoother than butter. Thankfully Leo had mentioned the hospital's unwillingness to give out patient information to anyone who wasn't kin. Greg *had* kin—retired parents in Arizona, a brother working for some company in Japan—but there was no one Rachel knew how to contact. If she wanted immediate answers on Greg's condition, she had to find some way to get them on her own.

And the fib worked—at least claiming to be his sister successfully got her transferred to another hospital floor. But then she was put on hold. And then transferred to yet another floor. One could interpret all this monkeying around as great news, she told herself. If they were moving him around, he was obviously alive, right? And he couldn't be in too bad a shape or he'd be immobilized in ICU. Yet her fingernails drummed a worried rhythm on the old yellow linoleum counter.

It seemed like she was stuck on hold for hours this time. A dozen memories of the lumbering, gentle giant flashed through her mind. She'd met Greg two years before, the day she'd moved into the neighborhood. He'd stopped by to welcome his new next-door neighbor. She'd nearly bitten his head off.

It hadn't been exactly her best day. Mark had just announced that he'd discovered "true love" with the bimbo. Rachel knew nothing about divorces then, had no idea you weren't supposed to leave the marital home—or the savings accounts—unarmed and undefended. She'd never lived anywhere but her hometown of Madison, but she'd impulsively taken off for Milwaukee because it seemed best. She didn't want to live in the same town as the cheating creep, and had craved a distance from her overprotective family, as well. This house was the cheapest rent she could find, at a time when even cheap was too expensive for her. She had no job, no money, an ego in shreds and a life in shambles. She never planned to trust another man as long as she lived.

She'd never planned on trusting Greg, either. But tarnation. He'd given her absolutely no choice.

"Ms. Martin?"

Finally a live body answered at the other end of the receiver, but the call proved worthless. Greg was still "undergoing tests." His condition was labeled "serious." No one would say exactly what his injuries were, or when he'd be settled down in a room and okayed for visitors.

Rachel heard out all the hospital rules, hung up, jammed the ice cream in the freezer and then simply hurled out of the house again for her car. Never mind their rules. Never mind anyone's rules. Greg had put her pieces back together when she thought she was too broken to mend. It wasn't his fault that he was one of the Enemy Species with that unfortunate Y chromosome. He was still the best friend she'd ever had—and nobody was going to stop her from seeing him.

Naturally St. John's was one of the oldest hospitals in the city, which naturally meant it was way downtown, which naturally meant she had no idea how to get there. She knew where to shop, how to locate the art and entertainment centers, could find Rudy's—the die-cast company where she worked as an engineering secretary—in her sleep. But Milwaukee's industrial section was a tangle of tanneries and foundries, railroads and shipping canals. Roasting hops from the downtown breweries added an alien, bitter smell to the humid night air. Rachel never had reason to become familiar with these inner-city neighborhoods—nor would she be driving them alone in the dark if she had a choice. Tonight, of course, she had no choice, but fear of getting lost only made her more anxious, and her tummy was already roiling with nerves.

By the time she was parked and galloping through the hospital's entrance doors, though, that problem was forgotten and another one nipping on her mind. If anyone questioned her claim about being Greg's sister, Rachel figured no one was going to believe her lie. Obviously lots of siblings looked dissimilar, but man, she and Greg were drastic opposites in physical appearance.

He was a hefty six foot three; she was five foot four—in heels. He had to tilt the scales past two hundred and fifty pounds, where she only weighed one hundred and ten if she wore a winter coat and clunky shoes. She was small-boned; he was a natural defensive end. Their personal styles were even more night and day. Greg often claimed that she looked like a younger Meg Ryan. That wasn't true—he was just being a sweetie—but she did have the blondish hair and blue eyes, and people had been annoyingly labeling her as girl-next-door "cute" since she was six. Greg…well. There was nothing wrong with his looks—nothing—but he wasn't exactly the kind of guy who cared about his appearance. His jet-black hair was whacked off in a dorky style; his glasses were usually broken, and his clothes looked like something twenty years out of date—and lacked all claim to taste even then.

Still, as she started asking questions at the hospital's front desk, no one seemed inclined to challenge her claim to be a relative. Possibly it helped that she looked so pitiful, with her limp hair straggling to her shoulders and her wilted suit and the run in her stocking. Who'd go out in public looking so wasted if they didn't have to? Cripes, she hadn't even stopped to put on lipstick. But it wasn't as if Greg would ever care or notice what she looked like. The only thing that mattered was finding him.

Questions eventually led her up one set of elevators, then down a mile-long hall, where she searched for room 315. Her spirits lifted just knowing he'd been settled in a regular room. At least he wasn't in surgery or worse. Maybe he was just a little battered up, she tried to reassure herself.

Only, her heart stopped when she poked her head through the doorway of room 315. The room looked like a clone of all the others—a mutated melon color, linoleum too ugly to wear out, inescapable antiseptic smells. It wasn't that bad. It was just the usual two-bed hospital room…and only the far bed by the window was occupied.

But the occupant in that bed was a long, long way from just "a little battered up."

She would never have recognized Greg at all, if it weren't for a glimpse of jet-black hair and the lumberjack shape under the sheets. She tiptoed closer with her heart in her throat. Bandages completely covered his face, except for a narrow strip around his eyes. He was connected to tubes all over the place. There was some kind of contraption affecting his jaw and neck. His left arm was raised on a pillow and immobilized in a splint.

"Hey."

Rachel almost jumped when she heard his voice. He was lying so still that she feared he was unconscious. But the kindest blue eyes in the universe had suddenly opened to half slits and looked drug-dazed. His normally strong tenor was barely a cracked, strained whisper.

"Hey, back." She plastered on her cheeriest smile and touched his right hand. She was afraid to touch anything else. She didn't want him to know how frightening he looked. "You can go right back to sleep, Stoner. I'm only going to stay a minute. I just had to know for sure how you were. And I'm not positive you should even be trying to talk—"

He motioned to the constraining bandages affecting his jaw. "I can talk—because nothing hurts. They just dosed me up with morphine. But I can't seem to speak any louder or clearer than this mumbling…and I guess I'll be eating dinner out of a straw for a while. Don't look so scared, Rach. Everything's mendable. I'll be fine."

Rachel wanted that promise in blood from a doctor. "This is a heck of a way to get time off work, you lazy slug."

"You know me. Any excuse to loll around."

Yeah, she knew him. He lumbered around with his glasses askew and a chronic distracted air, looking like the stereotype of a bumbling, absentminded professor. But it was so easy to misjudge Greg based on his appearance. The neighbors all camped out on his doorstep whenever there was a community problem, because he was just one of those people who quietly stepped up and took charge.

She'd learned that—firsthand—the day she moved in. Unfortunately there was no denying that she'd been a mortifying disaster that afternoon. The thing was, she'd married Mark with the foolish, naïve idea that marriage was forever, and discovering his relationship with the bimbo had emotionally leveled her. She'd taken off with a wild hodgepodge of belongings. A lamp, but no table to put it on. A mattress, but no bed. Her grandma's sacred red-velvet antique love seat, but no silverware. A few dishes, but nothing she could boil water in. Greg had asked if he could help her carry things. She'd snarled out a no.

He'd chosen to ignore her and simply started toting

things in, making trip after trip for no thanks. Eventually it became obvious—even to her—that a puppy could have packed better than she had. For all the stuff she'd mounded together, she lacked even the basics to get through a single day. She didn't have a broom, didn't have a spoon. And when she realized that she'd been so stupid as to even forget shoes—plenty of clothes, but no shoes beyond the pair on her feet—she'd plunked down on the porch steps and cried. Greg had plunked next to her and doled out tissue, as if coping with a rude, fruitcake neighbor having an out-of-control crying jag was nothing unusual in his day.

Looking at his white-bandaged face now made her feel fierce and angry. He'd been there for her so many times. She wanted to shoot whoever had done this to him, strangle them with her bare hands, *do* something. Not just because she owed him, but because she loved the big lug. "Are they giving you enough pain juice in those tubes?" she asked lightly.

"Too much. My head's in la la land. You don't have to stand there, Rach, sit…"

"I'll sit. For a minute. But I can't believe you need company for long. And I should probably confess that I'm not supposed to be here. I lied and told them I was your sister, so don't blow my cover, okay?"

"Okay, sis."

She wanted to chuckle. Even with the strange, strained sound of his voice, she could hear the hint of his dry humor. Through blizzards and power outages and crises, she'd never heard Greg lose his sense of humor. "I want to ask you how the accident happened, but I'm not still convinced that you should be talking. I don't understand exactly what kind of bandage contraption they've got around your jaw, but if it hurts you to talk—"

"It doesn't hurt. Nothing hurts. Like I said, I'm in poppy heaven. I just can't open my mouth very far. I think they wired my jaw, but I was really out of it a few hours ago and I'm honestly not sure exactly what anyone was doing to me in the E.R.''

She scooched a chair closer. "So you think your jaw's broken. Your arm, too?''

"Yeah, for sure on the arm. They just haven't set it yet. It was too swollen. The bone guy's supposed to come back and take a look still tonight.... Rachel?''

"What?'' His sudden hesitation, the way he said her name, made her quickly surge forward with alarm. "What can I do? Do you want water? The nurse?''

"No. I'd just feel better to get this said—you may not recognize me when this is over. There was a plastic surgeon in here earlier, too. He was pretty frank about the injuries to my face. He made out like they'll be rebuilding from scratch. Could be my days of being a handsome hunk are over.''

Rachel felt her heart clamp in a painful fist. She wanted to say the right thing, whatever would help him most, but she just didn't know what that was. Although the gauzy bandages completely concealed his expression, she could see those steady blue eyes searching hers. And he was joking about the "handsome hunk.'' Once Greg had wryly described himself as a fade-in-the-woodwork kind of guy. He was a comptroller, so it wasn't like he needed to be a *GQ* fashion plate. And since he chose the geeky haircut and dated clothes and never seemed concerned about the extra thirty pounds, Rachel had just assumed that looks didn't matter to him. Once she'd come to love him as a friend, she never thought about his physical appearance one way or another.

But she did now. This was way, way different. Maybe

Greg didn't have a vain bone in his body, but facing a drastic change in appearance was still a terribly unnerving thing to cope with. If he had to deal with scars, that was more disturbing yet. Although they'd never been the touchy-feely kind of friends, again she reached for his hand and loosely laced her fingers with his. "You know, if you get a new face, you could be even more drop-dead handsome than you are now."

"Well, hell. You think that's possible?"

She grinned. "Hopefully not, because I'm not sure I could survive living next door to that big ego, Stoner. With any luck, they'll let you keep a few scars, though. I don't know what it is about scars, but they either seem to appeal to a girl's pirate or bad-boy biker fantasy. You'll probably have to beat the women off with a stick."

"Not that. Not a fate worse than death. And how come I had to reach the vast age of thirty-two before I heard this interesting fact of life? Maybe you'd better explain some more about that biker fantasy—"

There was a hint of devil in his eyes, enough to make her chuckle. "Forget it. Women only tell those fantasies on a need-to-know basis. And you don't need to know anything else from me—particularly since I couldn't care less what you look like one way or another—but now you've got me thinking about this. Hey. You get a whole new face out of this deal? Where do I sign up?"

"Sheesh. Bite your tongue. You're cuter than Meg Ryan now. No way you ever need to touch that face."

"If you feel good enough to flirt, you can't be too bad off, Stoner. But we have to get serious, because any second now some nurse is bound to walk in and kick me out. I'm trying to think of what you need done." Rachel foraged in her purse for her checkbook—since she didn't have a pad of paper—and a pen. "All right. Now you know I have a key to your house, so I can do the obvious stuff—close the windows, take care of perishables in the fridge, get your mail—''

"I don't want to put you to any trouble."

"Don't be a goose. Look at all the stuff you did for me over the last two years." She ripped off a deposit slip, clicked on her pen and started to make a to-do list.

"Yeah, well, you didn't know a screwdriver from a hammer two years ago. But…if you don't mind, I'd appreciate your calling my work. Monica."

Monica Kaufman was the CEO where Greg worked as a comptroller, Rachel already knew. "Sure thing. And how about your parents? I don't know if you can make a long-distance call from a hospital room like this. You want me to call them?"

His eyes closed, as if he'd suddenly dropped off, just like that. But then he spoke again. "No. I need to contact them, if only so they know where I am. But they're both getting older, and I don't want to give them a shock or a scare if I don't have to. I'll find a way to call them myself—but not until I know from the docs exactly what's going to happen."

He still hadn't opened his eyes. She hesitated. "Greg, I don't want to stay, even another minute, if there's any chance you could fall asleep and really rest—''

"I'm not sleeping. It's just the drugs. I seem to keep zoning out and then somehow my mind starts replaying the accident.…"

"You want to talk about it, get it off your chest?"

Outside the door, carts wheeled by, nurses called, the loudspeakers kept snapping out codes. But inside Greg's room it was another world, a quiet, private world that only included the two of them. Their fingers had been loosely threaded together, but now his grip tightened until the heat of his palm nested in the heart-bed of hers. "I was in the old MG, not the Volvo. On I-94 in the middle lane, just driving back to work after lunch. That's all. Nothing weird. Only this truck ahead suddenly blew a front tire and he was swerving everywhere, all over the road...and so was everyone behind him, trying to clear out of his way. I was the peanut butter between a Cadillac and an Explorer. My MG squished like a pancake. Lucky."

He wasn't through talking, but his voice was losing power, sounding increasingly syrup-thick and slow. She leaned forward, clasping his hand more snugly. She'd never held hands with Greg—there'd never been even a teensy problem with male-female chemistry between them—and she felt embarrassed at her sudden awareness of his big fingers and maleness and the electric feeling of connection. Naturally, though, her emotions were nerves-sharpened. He was painfully describing how lucky he was to even be alive.

"Three other cars were in the same smash-up. At least nobody was killed. Took the Jaws of Life to get two of us out of our cars. I don't even know where all the glass came from. The back of the one truck, maybe. But it was the glass that cut up my face—could have my eyes so easily. And I kept hearing this little girl—she was crying. Rach? Will you find out how she is for me?"

"I'll ask, Greg. I promise."

"She was crying so hard, I told myself she had to be okay. I mean, nobody could bawl that loud if they weren't basically pretty strong. But find out, okay? She was so little."

It was so typical of Stoner, worrying about others. "I'll get an answer. But in the meantime, I think I should leave and you should rest. Only, before I come back tomorrow, can you think of some things you need me to bring? I assume you want your own toothbrush, but I don't know if you can use one if your jaw's all wired up—''

''Believe me, I'll find a way to use one. If I can't brush my teeth, I'd have to commit hara-kiri. So yeah, I really would appreciate that.''

''And you probably want your own pajamas—''

''Um, Rach. I don't do pajamas.''

''Oh. Well.'' She could feel a flush blooming on her cheeks and wanted to kick herself. At twenty-nine years old—and having been both married and divorced—it was downright ridiculous to fluster up at the idea of a man sleeping naked. Particularly when Greg was just a friend. ''Well, with all those bandages on your face, I don't think you'll be needing a razor for a while. I'll bring some books and magazines, but there must be something else I can do.'' Abruptly she snapped her fingers. ''I know what.''

''What?''

''Your sacred lawn. All life would end if it didn't get mowed by Saturday, wouldn't it? So I'll get your grass cut. I won't manicure it like you do, but consider this is an offer I wouldn't make to even Mel Gibson. Even Brad Pitt. We're talking a true test of how much I love you, neighbor. Now…what else could be worrying you?''

''Nothing.''

''Well, something else may cross your mind, but I'll come back and visit tomorrow after work. You can make a list if you think of anything else.''

His hand clutched hers just for a second longer, and then loosened. ''Rach—thanks for coming.''

''No sweat.'' But once she stood up, Rachel couldn't just leave. He looked so alone in that bed, so isolated behind the wall of bandages. And though he had dozens of friends, right then she felt like the only family he had.

There was simply no way that she could walk out of that room without expressing support and caring in some concrete, physical way.

So she bent down, but finding a spot to kiss him was almost a humorous challenge. His face and brow—and really, most of his head—were wrapped in white gauze. The only uncovered spot was his mouth.

His lips were naked, warm, soft. She snapped her head back up. Instantly. Not because she suddenly, inappropriately, felt her pulse buck and bolt—but because all she intended was a kiss lighter than the stroke of silk. Anything else risked hurting him. Anything else risked…well, this was Greg. Not just a good man, but a true hero of a friend. Rach would die if he misunderstood any gesture from her.

"All right, you," she said firmly. "I'm outa here. But I want you to behave yourself until I come back tomorrow—no seducing the nurses, no playing football in the hall, no wild drinking parties, you hear me? And I'll be in tomorrow right after work."

She made it outside in the hall, out of Greg's sight, before abandoning the cheerful smile and leaning weakly, sickly, against the wall. God. All those tubes. All those bandages. Sure, it could have been worse, but there was no question in her aching heart that he was lucky to be alive.

Without talking to a doctor, she had no idea what his prognosis really was. Or what he had to face ahead. The only thing Rachel felt sure of was fiercely wanting to be there for him.

Whatever it took to get him on his feet again, she was more than willing to do.

TWO

"And how's my gorgeous hunk doing today? Running around the halls naked again? Seducing all the nurses? Giving all the doctors hell?"

Greg's pulse stopped dead, then suddenly bolted faster than a runaway horse. For almost a month now, Rachel had visited at the same time every evening—but tonight she wasn't expected. And because he'd been so positive she wasn't coming, he had no time to mentally brace. For one vulnerable minisecond, the sound of her voice made his heart dip into that wild, wicked well of forbidden waters.

But that was just because he was in love with her.

By the time he turned his head to face her and started cranking up the bed to a sit-up posture, naturally he'd squashed the inappropriate emotion. It wasn't that hard to do, not anymore, particularly when he risked losing Rach altogether if she ever discovered how he felt about her. She was the princess to his frog. That's just the way it was, which he'd accepted ages ago. Still…after a man had been cooped up all day in a tediously monotonous hospital room, Rachel was like a burst of vital, vibrant stinging life.

Raindrops spattered everywhere as she stripped off her trench coat, revealing the suit and heels she'd worn to work. Knowing Rach, the suit couldn't have cost much, but she had this way of wearing clothes that made everything look expensive and sharp. Not flaunty. She didn't go for flashy styles that showed off her figure, yet typically this outfit was a subtle feast for his eyes. The suit was a soft cherry-red, with a slim skirt that palmed the curve of her fanny and a short jacket that bared a spot at her neck for jewelry. She did like her beads. Temporarily her tawny hair looked wind-tousled and shaggy—the way he liked it best—and framed a small face with giant blue eyes, an itsy nose and a generous, wide mouth. Rach hated the label of "cute," but man, she was. Darling. Cute. Irresistible. Words Greg never used on a woman, vocabulary he never used at all. Except for her. In the privacy of his mind.

"I've been giving everybody hell," he assured her. "One of these days, I figure it'll work and they'll throw me out of this place. But I didn't expect to be venting any bad temper on you tonight. Didn't you get the message on your answering machine? I called to tell you not to come."

"Yeah, I got your message about the weather. I just ignored you, big guy. What, did you think I'd melt if I drove in a little rain?"

It wasn't raining "a little." A harmless drizzle had started around noon, putting a shine and glisten on all the orange and gold autumn leaves, but by nightfall, the friendly little rain had turned into a gusty, moody storm. If and when all that water iced up, the roads would turn into a skating rink. "You're supposed to listen to the advice of your elders," Greg said sternly.

Her peal of laughter was infectious. "You don't get credit for being a mere three years older than me! And yeah, I know the roads may freeze, but the temperatures aren't supposed to drop that low until midnight. The nurses'll toss me out long before then." She kicked off her wet heels and padded closer to the bed in her stocking feet, her gaze narrowed as she studied him. "Well, I can't tell if they put you through any fresh torture today. Are you in pain?"

"Nope, I'm fine, really."

She rolled her eyes. "You always say that. And I think all those white bandages are mysterious and sexy and all, but I'm awfully sick of not being able to see your face, Stoner. I can't tell when you're lying. I can't tell when you're hurting or happy or anything else...."

As far as Greg was concerned, the only good thing to come from the accident were the bandages. Yeah, they were annoying, but at least Rach couldn't see his expressions. For a whole month now, he could look at her without worrying about giving away his true feelings for her.

"But you're finally at the end of this torture setup. I know you have to be feeling raw after the surgery yesterday, but this is the last time the plastic surgeon plans to cut you, yes? Didn't he promise? No more? So if you just heal from this sucker, you're home-free. I don't suppose they let you have solid food today?"

"No. And I'd rather have a cheeseburger right now than a million bucks. But at least that's the only blackmail they're still holding over my head. The minute I can keep down some solid food, I get to bump this pop stand and go home...only, that's tough to pull off when nobody's willing to bring me anything but a liquid dinner.''

Her soft eyes swam with sympathy. ''Now, Stoner. You know the broken jaw thing was the toughest problem, but you're on the total mend track now. It won't be that much longer.'' She shot him a teasing diamond-watt grin. ''Although I'm not sure I'm going to recognize you when this is all over. A whole new face is only part of this. You're practically down to skin and bones. No love handles. Only half of you to hug. We're talking about a woman's dream—you've lost so much weight that you're going to need a giant shopping trip to buy all new clothes.''

Temporarily he couldn't wince—but he wanted to. ''You call that a dream? I call it a nightmare. I'd rather have chicken pox than shop. I'd rather eat liver. Hell, I'd rather do anything.''

Rachel perched a hip on the bed and pulled the hospital tray table between them. A deck of cards appeared in her hands. ''Well, from the goodness of my heart, I'll help keep your mind off your troubles. You prepared to lose the rest of your life savings tonight?''

''Are you gonna fleece a poor, disadvantaged invalid *again?*''

''Yup. In fact, while you're on this losing streak, I think we should up the ante to maybe a dime a game instead of just a nickel.''

''There goes my retirement,'' Greg said plaintively, and was rewarded with her rich throaty chuckle.

Rach shuffled with the flashy style of a Las Vegas hustler and then dealt the cards. He cheated so she'd win— but no more than three out of four hands. If she won them all, Greg figured she'd guess something was fishy, particularly since he was a comptroller and should have had some skill with numbers.

His bumbling ineptitude didn't seem to trouble her, though, possibly because she loved winning. And since he loved watching her win, Greg considered them even. Tonight, besides, he really couldn't concentrate on the cutthroat canasta game.

His ribs still screamed when he laughed. The broken arm itched. And in the beginning, the bandages swathing his head had aroused his sense of humor—he *did* look like a mummy in training—but they also constricted his sight and movement and he was sick of them now. What the plastic surgeon had cut—and recut—on his face over the last weeks had involved constant bruising and swelling, and their rebuilding his jaw had been the worst. He couldn't eat, couldn't sleep, could never just let down and relax because there was always some kind of pain nagging at him.

But he forgot all that while Rach was here.

Thunder boomed outside. Rain slashed against the windows, running down the glass in silver ribbons. Against that black night, Rachel's skin looked pearl-soft and luminous, like a treasure a man felt compelled to protect—even if her eyes were full of the devil and she was unrepentantly trying to sneak a peek at his cards. "Are you saving aces over there, Stoner?"

"Like I'd tell you."

"I think you are." Again she peered into his eyes as if she could see the truth there. "You know I'm at a disadvantage because I can't see your face, when you can see mine. So I think it's only fair that you give me a hint whether you have an ace or two."

"Fair? Fair! You're talking to a man who's lost for four

nights running. I'll tell you whether I have aces when hell freezes over.''

She sniffed. ''Okay. When you get home, I was going to make you a big fat steak on the grill with French fries, because I thought that'd taste good after all the meals you've had to drink from a straw. But if you can't even give me a teensy little hint—''

''God. You play just like a girl. Sneaky. Manipulative. Making low-down blackmail threats—''

''Yeah. So what's your point?''

He let out an exhausted sigh. ''I have aces. Is that what you wanted to know?''

''Uh huh.'' She promptly dispensed a deuce—and a female-rascaly grin at the same time.

They kept playing…but Greg's mind couldn't help spinning back to the day he'd met her. She was full of frisky sass now, but not that day. That afternoon she'd reminded him of a kitten drenched in a storm. Miserable, huddled into herself, eyes shell-shocked and lost—but just like a cat, she spit and clawed if anyone tried to help her. Particularly anyone male.

She'd been married to Mark for seven years.

Two seconds after meeting Rach, Greg was inclined to murder the guy—and he didn't even know the whole story then. The details had drifted out over time. She'd still been wildly in love when her Sacred Mark walked out. She had no idea there was another woman in the picture. She had no clue there was even a problem. They hadn't argued. He hadn't complained. She was under the impression their sex life was superb.

From the start of the relationship, Rach had dropped out of college to put her True Love through school. Then she'd worked two low-wage jobs while the spineless jerk was getting around to sending out résumés. Her turn to finish college somehow never happened. Mark-O just had a lot of needs—like the right clothes and wheels suitable to a certain status, then the right house in the right neighborhood, and naturally he couldn't sacrifice any fishing or hunting trips with his pals.

Greg figured that Rach had had plenty of clues early on. She just hadn't wanted to see that her Sacred Mark was a selfish, immature jerk. Actually, to a point, Greg didn't think that particularly mattered. If she loved the guy, then she did.

But what killed Greg—what fried him upside and down the other—was that the son of a bitch had broken her heart. Mark had obviously been the only guy she ever loved, ever knew intimately. His chasing another woman had the same effect as ripping the heart right out of her. The day she'd moved next door, she'd had nothing—a checkbook with a couple hundred dollars, no job, no plans, and a little rented U-Haul heaped with impractical, sentimental junk that she couldn't even sell, much less wear or eat.

Greg had never felt it happen before. His heart, doing the slam-bam-alakazaam thing. His hormones, suffering instant delirium. His nerves, trying to electrocute him with the lightning-bolt voltage.

Of course she wasn't for him. Greg recognized that right off. Look what happened when King Kong pined after the blonde. When Romeo started moping after a Capulet. When Bogart got obsessed with a married woman in *Casablanca*. When a guy fell in love with an inappropriate woman, nothing ever followed but a heart-gashed-in-two and disaster. There was love and there was *love*. If you had the wrong kind, best you bite the bullet, shut up and just try to value what you did have.

"I'm *out*." Rachel—the fragile, withdrawn, vulnerable

woman he'd fallen in love with—snapped down her last
card and then wiggled her fingers. "Gimme, gimme,
gimme. Thirty whole cents. Am I good or am I good?
You might as well admit it, Stoner. I buried you. I
trounced you *deep*. I beat the pants off you."

"You're the worst winner I ever met, " he grumbled,
and dug in the bedside table for his wallet. "You ever
hear of the word *humble?*"

"What's to be humble for? I won, I won, I won."

He couldn't grin because of the bandages. He couldn't
laugh because of the sore ribs. But he wanted to do both.
As he forked over her thirty cents, he savored how much
she'd changed from two years ago. For a while, Greg had
his doubts she'd ever recover from the blows that creep
had inflicted on her.

One of the rehab staff—a buxom nurse named Maeve—
cocked her head through the doorway. "Well, if this isn't
typical. Visiting hours are over. The whole floor's quieted
down. All my good patients are behaving themselves. And
then there's you two."

Rachel chuckled, but she also swiftly scooched off the
bed. "I'm sorry. And I promise, I'm leaving right away."
The nurse had barely disappeared before she added to
Greg, "I'll give you a chance to earn back the loot tomorrow."

"You'd better," he said with the tone of the longsuf-
fering.

With a cheeky grin, she started searching for her shoes
and found them lying cockeyed under the chair. "You
know what?"

"What?"

She pushed on the shoes, then grabbed her trench coat.
"Every day you've sounded stronger, Greg, but tonight
was the first time that you really, really sounded like your-

self. I realize you're not quite ready to climb K-2, and those bandages still make you look like one of those Egyptian pharaoh mummies. But I think they just might let you out of here soon."

"That's exactly what I told the doc this morning. It's time to throw me out. Tomorrow wouldn't be too soon for me."

"I don't blame you for being impatient. If I'd been cooped up this long, I'd be going just as nuts. But this started out almost as scary as the Humpty Dumpty story, Stoner. They had a lot of pieces to put back together." She cinched the belt on her trench coat and then clipped toward him. "Just for the record, I *am* going to make you that steak and French fries as soon as you get home. You just have to stay cool a little longer and do what the docs tell you, okay?"

She bent down. He saw her wispy bangs, the faint spray of freckles on her nose, her soft mouth. He knew she was going to kiss him. Before the accident, she'd never touched him, but she'd pulled this kiss-good-night routine fairly often since he'd been in the hospital.

Now, like those other times, her lips had to search for a spot to kiss because almost everything above his neck was covered with white gauze.

Now, like the other times, her blue eyes flashed on his first. For two years Rach had been allergic to men, never went out, never gave a guy a chance to hurt her. Greg was positive that he'd earned her trust, yet still she needed to do that affirming quick eye study to remind herself that he was different—a proven friend, not a predator, not a male where sex or intimacy was an issue.

Now, like the other times, she seemed to decide it was okay to express an honest affectionate gesture with him...and did. Her lips touched down, softer than satin, gentler than a sigh. He caught the faint drift of the spicy scent she wore, saw her silky blond hair sweep down in pale, fine curls, inhaled the rustle of girl clothes and the pure delicate femaleness of her. And the first time she'd kissed him, all he had to do was brace because it was all over in two seconds.

But now, like the other times, Rach seemed to unconsciously stretch it out. Past two seconds.

Past five.

Past the point of a good-night-smack between pals, although Greg was meticulously careful not to touch her, not to move, not to breathe.

When she finally lifted her head and straightened up, her eyes flashed on his again, then swiftly shifted away like a nervous gambler's. Color streaked her cheeks. Her hands restlessly tightened a belt that was already securely tied.

"You really need to get out of here." Greg covered the sudden awkward silence. "I'm going to worry about your driving on ice if you don't get home."

That coaxed back her natural smile again. "I'm going, I'm going." She snatched up her purse and hiked toward the door. "Give the nurses hell, I love you and sleep good, okay?"

Once those orders were delivered, naturally she whisked out of the room before he could respond. For a few seconds longer he could hear her heels clicking down the hospital linoleum, and then she was gone. Greg sank against the pillow and squeezed his eyes closed. It was worrisome. Not just her recent habit of kissing him, but her brand new habit of leaving him with that light, blithe, "I love you."

Only a few moments passed before Maeve ambled back in. "Hi, darlin'. Your company finally gone?"

"Yes."

"As many visitors as you get, she's my favorite. Such a sweetie. And cute as a button." Efficiently Maeve wrapped his arm in the blood pressure cuff, then did the temperature and the pulse routine. "I got a secret for you. Dr. Webster says we can try you on real food tomorrow. And if that goes okay, you'll be out of here in a matter of days. Now I've got some juice and couple of pills for you...."

Greg sipped the juice, ignored the pills, and when Maeve had moved on to badger the patient in the next room, he twisted to a sitting position and slowly stood up. He made it the five steps to the window, but the sensation of dizzy weakness was exasperating.

All the broken parts on his torso were healing fine. It was his face that had kept him trapped in the hospital all these weeks. From the broken jaw to the reconstruction surgeries, he'd been drinking dinners for weeks now. He could do physical therapy, but he simply could not build up strength when his diet maxed out at soft foods like tapioca.

Bracing both hands on the windowsill, Greg scanned the rain-slick parking lot below, hoping to spot Rachel. Headlights blinked and glared, but it was too dark to identify any cars, even anything as distinctive as her classic-survivor yellow VW. He was about to give up and step away, when he caught his mirror reflection in the glass pane.

The tall, lean man in the reflection was stunningly— eerily—unfamiliar. Yeah, he'd always been tall, but even from childhood, he'd been chunky and stoop-shouldered. Now his body felt like a stranger's. The new lean build and straight posture just didn't feel like him, and he was increasingly edgy about the mystery face under the bandages. The plastic surgeon had repeatedly promised him that the reconstruction surgeries had gone "fabulous" and he was going to look great. Truthfully, Greg didn't care what he looked like, as long as he didn't have scars that would scare children or draw attention to himself.

But suddenly he did care.

Something was happening between him and Rachel. Something new, something different. Something threatening. She just wasn't behaving the same around him. Sooner or later Rach was always going to realize that she wasn't allergic to men anymore, that Sacred Mark hadn't wounded her for life, that sleeping alone wasn't any fun for grown-ups. Greg had loved helping her. Loved feeling a part of her healing. Loved knowing he was one of the few men in the universe that she trusted.

But once he got home from the hospital, he just wanted to feel sure their next-door friendship went back to the way it was. He was the frog. She was the princess. Everything had always gone well between them as long as Greg never tried coloring outside those lines.

Slowly he turned around, then went through all the stiff contortions it took to get himself ready for bed and covered up again. Once the lights were off, he stared at the black ceiling, remembering Randall Conrad, the class bully in fourth grade. Greg had taken one beating from the bully and never told. Then another beating. It seemed that was around the time he started wolfing down extra snacks, playing the bumbling brain, making good-natured jokes no matter what anyone said to him. Randall had quit hounding him. Nobody had really picked on him after that.

In fact, girls had always liked him. Greg couldn't remember a time when he didn't have close female friends. He didn't threaten women. Didn't inspire them either—

but Greg knew himself incapable of doing that. By age thirty-two, naturally he'd had some serious relationships. If none had ended in marriage, none had ended badly or cruelly, either. They just seemed to fizzle out like champagne left uncorked. Personally, he never thought sex was worth all the hoopla. He seemed to bore the lovers he'd chosen, almost as badly as they'd bored him. He'd like to marry sometime. He'd like kids, like a family. But just to have another body in the house was no justification to pursue something where Greg had already proven to be mediocre.

Unlike the old song claimed, one wasn't the loneliest number. Two was. Being with someone you really didn't want to be with was not only exhausting, but the most painful brand of loneliness.

Greg was pretty sure Rachel felt nothing but sympathy for him. He was also pretty sure she had no clue he was in love with her. Her sympathy should die a natural death once he got home and back to normal life again, but he treasured their friendship and worried doing anything to screw it up.

The second he met Rachel, he'd known she wasn't for him. He had money. He had brains. But he'd never had the kind of zesty style and people skills and innate guts for life that she had. She'd shoot him for using the word *class* but there it was. It'd be like trying to pair a Chevy with a Jag. A guy could admire a Jag. Could lust after it. Could look. But a grown man with character knew better than to touch something that couldn't belong to him.

Greg sighed heavily and closed his eyes. Most of his life he'd been invisible, the kind of guy who faded into the woodwork and no one noticed. Other men liked attention. Not him. And right now all he wanted was to be home again—back to his work, back to his life, back to being comfortably invisible. Especially with Rachel.

A week later, Rachel rapped on Greg's back door, and when no one answered, she twisted the knob and poked her head inside. "Stoner! It's me, Rach! Are you here?"

"Yeah, I'm back here in the den."

Shaking her head with impatience, she stomped inside and closed the door. Technically Greg was still on a medical leave of absence, but there was no telling him that. When the hospital finally sprang him four days ago, he'd had a co-worker bring him work from the office ever since. He was *always* in the den working on the computer. Reminding him that he still had a doctor's mandate to take it seriously easy fell on deaf ears.

Quickly she peeled off her pea coat and tossed it on a kitchen chair, automatically glancing around the room. No crumbs cluttered the red-tile counter; no dishes were stacked in the white porcelain sink. Old-fashioned glass cabinets revealed neatly stacked plates, and the long oak table held a nauseatingly tidy pile of mail and magazines. Personally Rachel didn't trust anyone who didn't leave a shameful mess somewhere—it just wasn't human—but Greg was a friend. One had to forgive a friend a few revolting habits.

Momentarily, though, she only glanced around the kitchen to ascertain how he was doing today.

The dimwit wouldn't ask for help if his life depended on it, so Rachel had to rely on clues. He'd been working too hard ever since coming home from the hospital, but Stoner was too much of a hard-core perfectionist to ever leave a mess unless he were exhausted or in pain. Today, his spotless kitchen reassured her that he was feeling good.

Pushing off her shoes, she padded in stocking feet down the wainscotted hall and through the living room. His decor always struck her sense of humor. Greg had told her that Stoners had built the family home in the 1890s, and some furnishings were obviously heirlooms from that elegant Victorian period—like the mahogany breakfront and a burgundy crushed-velvet rocker and the rich Oriental rugs. And then there were Greg's choices. Futuristic minimalist. A spear of a lamp, a lapis lazuli slab for a coffee table, a giant wall-size TV and entertainment center, futons for seating. The furnishings were backdropped by old fashioned stuccoed walls and fancy copper-carved ceilings.

Rachel was unsure whether Greg didn't realize that nothing went together or, worse, that he thought it did. A wolf had to have a better sense of style that he did. The French doors at the far end of the living room opened onto his study.

She paused in the study doorway. The closed wooden blinds sealed out the midday sun and made the room murky-dim. All she could really see was Greg's back, hunched over a glowing computer monitor, his fingers clicking on the keyboard. He was wearing his favorite Green Bay sweatshirt—which was so decrepitly frayed that it should have seen a trash bin up-close-and-personal years ago—and he was obviously concentrating hard. One look, and a lump filled her throat.

She'd loved him as a friend for ages now, but feelings had hugely and drastically changed since his car accident. Maybe it was watching him cope with so much pain. Maybe it was all those nights in the hospital, the way he teased her, the way he cheated at cards so she'd win, the way they so easily laughed together.

Somehow she had just never looked at Greg as a *man*

before. She'd seen him as a brainy, overweight nerd, because that was how he'd always made such a point of billing himself. And more privately she'd thought of him as a gentle giant, because that's how he'd been with her—a neighbor, a friend, a fixer of fuses and a stealer of cookies and an unbeatable listener. She'd seen Greg in lots of roles. All of them wonderful.

But until the accident, she'd just never thought of him as a sexual being. A sexual single male human being.

Rachel wasn't positive she *wanted* to see him that way. To risk screwing up the best friendship she'd ever had troubled her. But in the silence of her heart, she couldn't deny that just being in the same room with him aroused emotions that had never been there before.

"Hey, slugger. You've got a doctor's appointment today. Did you forget?"

Greg didn't turn his head, didn't lift his fingers from the keyboard. "I didn't forget. The appointment's at one."

She came up behind him, her hands instinctively molding around his shoulders and neck. As she might have expected, his muscles were all knotted up. No question he'd been sitting here a long time. She started kneading, careful not to touch the bandages wrapped around his head. "And do you know what time it is right now, Stoner?"

"I dunno. Nine? Ten? God, that feels good, don't stop."

"It's noon." Her fingers dug and probed, trying to relax the knots in his neck. She'd have volunteered such a back rub for any ailing friend—male or female—only Rachel knew it wasn't the same. Not with him, not anymore.

As if her female hormones had suddenly come awake

after a two-year hibernation, she felt conscious of the warmth and scent of his skin, of her sensitized response to everything male about him. And that was wonderful, but also unnerving. She might have missed sex, but she really hadn't wanted to touch a man in all this time. And because Mark was the only man she'd known—no matter how much he'd hurt her—she'd just never anticipated touching any man intimately but him, either. Now, suddenly, she could imagine all kinds of disastrously wild and inappropriately naked things. With Greg. And once her mind started dripping those ideas, it seemed the leak just kept getting bigger.

"It can't be noon," Greg corrected her.

"Yeah, it is—12:02, actually. I don't know how you could possibly forget a red-letter doctor's appointment like this one—*finally* you're getting those bandages off your face after all this time—"

"I didn't forget. It's just I started working after breakfast—"

"And lost track of the time, I know." The knots had eased, which obliterated the judicious excuse she had for touching him. She dropped her hands. "If you want some company," she said casually, "I could drive you to the doc's. Friday's my home day at work, but I'm all caught up, so taking off a couple hours this afternoon is no problem."

"Nah. Thanks for offering, Rach, but really, that'd be crazy for you to waste your time sitting in a doctor's waiting room. There's no pain or anything like that involved where I'd have trouble driving alone."

"I know you have some trouble with visibility because of the bandages—"

"Yeah, I do. But it's just a fifteen minute drive there, and then these confounded bandages are off for good. I'll be fine, really.'' He still hadn't turned around and faced her, because he was still saving and messing with disks and then exiting the computer.

And she hesitated. If Greg didn't want her help, then he didn't. But she was still concerned about his going to this doctor's visit alone. Even for a man as unvain and totally oblivious to appearances as Greg, this afternoon was a huge traumatic thing.

The plastic surgeon had said over and over that the reconstruction surgeries had been successful...but Greg still really didn't know what he was going to look like. The doctor had given him computerized pictures approximating his new face, but that was it. Because he never talked about it, Rachel suspected Greg was just being Greg—a man who never thought much about looks. And maybe it was going to be that easy, but she wasn't convinced anyone could go through a traumatic change of appearance and not feel unsettled. She just wanted to go with him, to be there, to show him positively that she didn't give a royal damn what he looked like and he'd always be Greg to her.

But now he finished exiting his computer and spun around. ''Well, if you aren't a sight for sore eyes....''

She grinned. Okay, so the jeans were a little baggy and her yellow sweatshirt had seen better days. ''I was raking leaves this morning. I think every tree on the block dumped its leaves last night—and mostly in my yard and yours. Actually, I was thinking about raking your leaves after mine—''

''I can do my own.''

''Quit with the pride nonsense, Stoner. Just because you've got the cast off your arm doesn't mean you have any strength yet—either in your arm or your ribs. You're not up for heavy physical work and you know it. But for the record, I was going to put on a decent sweater if you'd let me drive you to the doc's office so you wouldn't be ashamed to be seen with me—''

''I couldn't be ashamed to be seen with you in this life, Rach.''

Maybe, but she couldn't talk him into letting her drive him, so she skedaddled home to give him time to get ready and go. She noted him leaving around 12:40 while she was putting together a cheese-and-tomato sandwich for lunch. As of one o'clock, she couldn't sit—she was too worried about the outcome of this doc's visit and what Greg might be thinking when the bandages came off—so she yanked on her old barn jacket and headed outside again with a rake.

Her yard was finished by one-thirty, and she unlatched the white rail fence gate into his. Between a century-old walnut and several maple trees in the back, his yard was a sea of apricot and russet leaves—way more than he could possibly handle alone. The leaves crunched and crackled under the pull of her rake. She made little piles. And then bigger piles. And still Greg didn't come home, not by two o'clock, not by two-thirty.

Her muscles were screaming by then, but how could she leave? If she stopped by later, Greg could think she only wanted a look at his face. As long as she kept raking, she had a legitimate excuse for being here. And finally, just before three, his black Volvo pulled into the driveway. She had already straightened, had already locked a welcome-hello smile on her face, when he climbed out of the car and faced her.

Her intention was absolute. No matter what Greg looked like, she wanted to say the right thing, the supportive thing—whatever it took to make him believe she was natural with his new appearance.

But "Oh my God" slipped out of her mouth before she could stop it. She was prepared for scars. She was prepared for him to look really different. She was prepared for Greg to need some help coping if the physical changes were disturbing.

But the look of his face was still a total and complete shock.

Three

——

Greg expected Rachel to notice his "new" face. It's not like anyone who knew him could possibly fail to notice. But she looked so stunned that he felt an edgy, uneasy lump well in his throat. "Rach, I'm not going to look like this forever. It's just going to take a while before the last of the swelling and bruises go down—"

"It's not the bruises or the swelling." Rachel plunked down on his front porch step as if she were too weak to stay upright. Knuckles cocked up her chin. Those velvet-blue eyes of hers seemed glued on his face. A siren screamed in the distance. She didn't look away. Kids ran down the sidewalk, yelling to each other. She didn't look away. The paper boy biked up, hurled the newspaper right past her head to his porch, and that didn't make her blink, either. "I just wouldn't know you. If I hadn't recognized your black Volvo pulling in the drive, I'd have thought you were a stranger."

"Yeah? Well, it's just me."

"Stoner. I just can't get over it. You're *gorgeous*." Her hand shot to her heart. She obviously worried that she had unintentionally hurt his feelings, because she backpedaled immediately. "Not that you weren't an incredibly good-looking sexy hunk before, but—"

"Rach, it's okay. Don't worry about saying something awkward. Believe me, I feel awkward myself." And that was an understatement, Greg thought irritably. He'd felt sledge-hammered the instant he saw his new face in the doctor's office mirror. Whether the damn face was ugly or handsome was irrelevant. The problem was that it wasn't *him*. It wasn't the face he'd grown up with. It wasn't anyone he recognized. And it was the eeriest sensation to be walking around with a stranger's face.

"A little unnerving to look so different?" Rachel said gently. "But you do look wonderful, Greg. I don't even see any scars except for the one on your forehead...."

"There are plenty of scars, but the doc did a good job putting most of them under my chin or around the hairline. Especially since I haven't had a haircut since the accident, most of those scars don't show. In fact, that's what the doc suggested—just wear my hair longer, like it is now." Greg could hear the restless, impatient tone creep into his voice again, but he couldn't help it. The doc's advice was fine, but all that unruly, thick hair hanging around his collar and forehead was another weirdness. He'd always worn his hair ultrashort. Maybe the style had been a little dorklike, but it took no care or maintenance beyond remembering to have a barber chop it off every few weeks. Hell, he hadn't even known he *had* all this hair.

Since this was Rach, though, he tried to erase the impatient frustration in his voice and make a joke out of the

situation. ''I stopped for gas on the way home. Same sta-
tion I've gone to for years, and Maurie didn't even recognize me. I feel like I walked into the doctor's office
being me, and came out starring in an *X-Files* episode.
Maybe the truth is out there, but this alien just isn't me.''

Instead of chuckling, like he intended her to, Rachel
slowly stood up with a thoughtful expression. ''I was
afraid this'd be harder than you expected. To a point, it's
different for women. We go for makeovers and new hair-
styles all the time. We love that stuff. Change is a way
to give us an emotional lift. But hair grows back, and we
can use our old eye shadow if we don't like the new
colors. But it's a whole different thing when you're not
choosing to change and never had a vote in it. Let's see
that forehead scar....''

She stepped closer, raising her hand to push aside his
hair near the right temple. Greg knew what she saw. On
the underside of his jaw were the newest and rawest-
looking scars. His eyes still had a raccoon look with the
bruising, and a jagged, skinny scar bisected his right eye-
brow. His jaw really throbbed and the nerve endings felt
hypersensitive, finally exposed to light and air, but nothing was really that horrible to look at. It was just different.
His chin was square now. He had a Frenchman's aquiline
nose. The cheekbones were still his, but they looked completely different in a face that used to be shaped full and
pudgy, and now looked sculpted with a decisive, strong
brush.

The plastic surgeon had been ecstatic with his finished
product.

Greg had no time to decide what he thought of the new
face yet—but he knew *precisely* what he felt about Rachel
being this close. His pulse responsively bucked for the
sparest, barest touch of her fingertips.

He told himself that a guy couldn't help reacting to a woman who was so sensitive to his feelings—but that was a total lie. Yeah, she was perceptive, and yeah, her kindness was a wonderful quality. But his hormones had always gone into a delicious dither anywhere around her.

He tried to analyze the problem. The way Rachel touched his forehead was obviously intended as a friendly, caring, but specifically nonsexual gesture. He understood that. It just didn't matter to his hormones.

His whole damn world still suffered a complete metamorphosis solely because of her nearness. Hours earlier he'd noticed the gunmetal-gray clouds festering in the west, likely swollen with snow this late in the fall. Yet now he saw the sun spearing down in a gold-kissed haze on the brilliant tangerine and magenta leaves. Before, the wind seemed mean-cold and now felt spanking fresh and invigorating. Suddenly he could smell leaves and pumpkins, cider and cinnamon, the leather and wool of coats— maybe all those autumn scents had been there before, but he hadn't noticed. And his hormones—the ones that had always been content to snooze through most male-female events—suddenly woke up and wanted to party.

Rachel dropped her hand and rocked back down on her heels, but her gaze still focused on his face in a studying way. "I'm not sure you're even going to have any scars when it's all healed, but right now you've still got places that look really painful," she said gently. "The stitch marks, for one. But also, even though the swelling and bruising is way down, you have to still be feeling tender."

"It's nothing."

"Maybe it's small-potatoes-pain compared to what you've been through these last weeks. But it's still not nothing. And I think it's a good thing you're not due back at work for another week yet."

"Rach—?"

"What?"

He had a question he wanted to ask her, but somehow it completely flew out of his mind. The thing was, she was still standing close. Nothing fancy about her play clothes; she was just wearing an old barn jacket and jeans and boots, but everything about her was beautiful to him. The wind had put rouge in her cheeks, and her eyes always did look softer than velvet, and the breeze was teasing her hair, making those honey-blond strands flutter and curl around her face. She just looked...kissable.

And suddenly he remembered all those kisses she'd tortured him with in the hospital. Every time he'd had bandages and casts and tubes trapping him. He could never touch her back. He could never kiss her back.

And of course, he wouldn't have, anyway. Kissing her was on his conscience's Absolute Forbidden list—the kind of list a man wrote in ink so he couldn't erase it. Still, now, he knew in exquisite detail what her small mouth tasted like. It was impossible not to wonder how a kiss might be without the bandages, without the casts and traction, when he could actually touch her.

"Stoner, what's wrong?"

"Nothing." Except for realizing he'd been staring at her like a robber let loose in a bank vault. Mentally he gave himself a whack upside the head.

Rachel cocked her head in confusion. "You started to ask me a question, but then you seemed to go off daydreaming—"

"I wasn't daydreaming. This was just a real awkward question to ask you." He needed to dissemble quickly, and did. He just also swiftly looked away so she couldn't see what was in his eyes. "You've done so much for me in the last few weeks, that I really hate to ask for a favor—''

''Oh, come on, you doofus. I've told you a zillion times. I really felt uncomfortable because of all the stuff you'd done for me since I moved here, and my never having a chance to pay you back. What can I do?''

''Well...'' Aw, hell. He might as well spit it out. ''I've been wearing a sweatshirt and sweatpants since I came home from the hospital...not just because those clothes are comfortable, but because it seems to be all I've got. One more week and I expect to go back to work—and really I could now, for a couple hours a day. But I must have lost a ton of weight in the hospital because nothing fits. Not suits, not pants, not anything. Even my shirts look like a clown's swimming in 'em.''

''Oh, God. Now I realize what you're facing.'' She gasped, and dramatically pressed her hand to her heart. ''This is worse than torture. Worse than your scariest nightmare. Worst than a fate worst than death. You're actually going to have to go *shopping?*''

He winced. ''Now, there's no reason we have to say that *S* word out loud. And I was hoping you might listen to an idea.''

''Believe me, I'm listening.'' Nothing, but nothing, beat one of those pure-female grins of hers.

''Well...my idea is that I could keep my poor, battered, recovering body at home. And you could do the shopping thing for me.'' He barreled on. ''For which, of course, I'd be willing to do about anything. You want me to pay a year's worth of rent? How about some jewels or doodads? Or how about a couple weeks in Tahiti...? Hey. Quit laughing. This is a serious business deal I'm offering you—''

She only chuckled harder at his aggrieved tone. ''You

know darn well I'll help you. You don't have to bribe me. But honestly, Stoner, you're getting more and more pitiful about this. It's not like you'd *die* if you had to walk into a department store.''

"You think I'm afraid of dying? Who was the guy who came over in the middle of the night because you were shrieking on the phone about a skunk in your backyard? I can do the courage thing any old time. This is entirely different. We're talking an evolutionary issue here. Shopping goes against the entire survival instinct for the male of the species.''

"I can't *wait* to hear you explain that.''

"I'm serious. Think about it. Nature gave each gender certain aptitudes to ensure the species' survival. The guys were supposed to go out and hunt and bring home the meat. That's why we need a remote control—using that trigger finger is just instinctive. And girls were the nest makers. That's why you females like shopping. You're collecting the junk to make the nest—but it's also why guys aren't supposed to shop. It's contrary to all the evolutionary laws of survival. I'm supposed to bring home the bacon—but you're supposed to buy the frying pan.''

"Stop. I can't take any more of this bologna.'' She raised a hand in a gesture pleading for mercy. "I give up. It'll take a bigger woman than me to knock that sexist attitude out of you—besides which, you already know perfectly well that I love shopping.''

"That did occur to me,'' he said gravely. "Mostly because I've noticed you have to go to fifty stores spread out over two states and seven or eight malls just to pick out a pair of jeans—''

She socked him. Gently. But then he got the royal finger wagged in his face. "Quit. You have to get serious for a minute, and I mean it. I'll be glad to shop for you,

Stoner, but I can't just *go*. I need a specific list of what you need—''

"You don't need a list. Just get some suits and shirts and stuff. You know. Things that guys wear who work in finance. If it's blue or gray, it's probably okay."

"I'll take your color preferences under advisement," she said dryly. "In the meantime, if you want me to do this, I will. But you still have to go to a tailor's with me, just one time—''

"Hell. Why?" he asked plaintively.

"To get fitted. I don't know what sizes you are. And you've lost so much weight, you couldn't know your sizes, either—plus, a suit isn't something you just buy off a hanger. The pants have to be hemmed. Sometimes stuff needs a tuck here or there. If a tailor'd measure you once, I think it'd be enough—now, don't give me that look. I'm telling you there's no other way to get it right. And in the meantime, how do you want me to pay for these clothes?"

"Hell, I don't know. How about if I just give you all the credit cards I own?"

"Now, come on, you. I need a serious answer."

Greg's eyebrows arched in surprise. "That *was* a serious answer."

He could have happily teased her for another couple hours, but at this time of year the sun dropped faster than a stone. Suddenly the wind picked up teeth and the daylight dissolved into a murky dusk. Rachel called off their discussion and hiked next door to her house—but not before throwing her arms in the air and disgustedly muttering "Men!" loud enough to make sure he heard. He heard. And chuckled all the way inside, where he ambled immediately to the kitchen window over his sink.

He could see Rachel's kitchen from that window. Saw her lights go on, saw her fly by in the barn jacket, then fly back a few moments later with the jacket gone, pushing up the sleeves of a snug yellow sweater as she opened her fridge. All summer, mouth-watering aromas had wafted from her open kitchen windows. She claimed to hate cooking, but she could bring a man to his knees on the aromas coming out of her pots any day of the week.

Hell, she could bring a man to his knees with one of her smiles, Greg mused. And for the first time all day, he relaxed.

For weeks now, his whole life had been dominated by the accident, and he'd had it. He was sick to death of feeling exhausted and weak all the time, bored with being unable to do the work he loved, and the whole business of getting a new face was tedious and nerve-racking. More troubling than all those things, though, had been the chronic, nagging worry that Rachel would never be comfortable with him again the way she was before.

He pushed away from the counter and opened his own refrigerator, prowling the shelves for dinner, feeling reassured about the only problem on that list that really mattered.

It was true that he'd lost a ton of weight and needed new clothes—but not true that he needed to bug Rachel into shopping for him. He hadn't asked to impose on her, but to reestablish himself as a nerd in her eyes—the guy who never noticed how he looked. The bookworm guy who was brainy with numbers but bumbling with people. The guy she never worried about trusting. And the whole shopping conversation thing had helped, Greg thought.

She was smiling at him again. Smiling, bantering, teasing him—just like she used to. She hadn't done anything petrifying like kiss him today. She hadn't given him any more of those alarmingly sexual looks.

Greg wanted her in his life. More than he wanted anything. But he'd always understood that Rach only encouraged the friendship because she saw him as safe and nonthreatening. His appearance was definitely part of that. He never wanted to appear *ugly* to her, but he'd always understood that an uncool, nerdy type of look effectively separated him from the men she considered potential dates. It would screw up everything if she realized he had sexual feelings for her.

And he was determined that would never happen.

On Friday night, Rachel was pacing in front of her living room when she finally saw Greg's Volvo pull into his driveway. She waited anxiously, trying to give him enough time to get in the house and turn on some lights before dialing next door.

"Greg? I was hoping to catch up with you tonight. I've got your clothes. Of course your credit card's going to rival the national debt, but I warned you about that beforehand—"

She heard a chuckle rumble out of his throat, then his lazy, easy baritone. "Hey, I told you I didn't care what it cost. I'm just grateful you were willing to do this. You want me to come over and get the clothes off your hands now?"

"Yes, if you can. The thing is, if you try the clothes on tonight and you either don't like some things or they don't fit, I'll have time to return them tomorrow. But I'm going out tonight, so unless you can come over in the next hour..."

"No problem, Rach. I'll be there in two shakes."

The instant she hung up, Rachel restlessly tugged on an earring. She wasn't nervous about seeing him, she told herself. That thought was ridiculous, considering how long they'd known each other. She was just feeling a little anxious because of her shopping spree. She'd only purchased what she thought Greg seriously needed. That's it. No more, no less. It was just a teensy bit conceivable that Stoner might suffer a heart attack when he saw the packages liberally heaped in her living room—not to mention his response when he saw the styles and colors she'd picked out.

Seconds later, Greg rapped his knuckles on her back door and then ambled into her kitchen. "Hi, you."

"Hi, you back." One look at Greg's new face and she forgot the guilt, forgot what she'd blissfully done to his platinum credit card, forgot her own name. Holy molly. It was just impossible to get used to. Greg wasn't just gorgeous. He was a downright stunning hunk.

But Rachel swiftly steeled her expression into a casual welcome-hi smile, not wanting him to realize how much his changed appearance affected her. The other day he'd made very clear how uncomfortable he felt about his new face. As his friend, she wanted to help him, not add to his discomfort—or ever give him the impression she was the kind of shallow person who cared about looks. She didn't. She really didn't. Only, tarnation, for two years she'd lived next door to a lumbering, overweight giant and suddenly he'd metamorphosed into a lean, mean George Clooney.

"All your loot's in the living room—come on in," she said, only to have him yank off his jacket, take one long slow look at her and tease her with a wolf whistle.

"I'll be damned. I thought you were fibbing. You really are going out? Don't tell me we're talking a hot date. Don't tell me Ms. Celibate-For-The-Rest-Of-Her-Life Martin is actually going to do the wild thing and go out on a Friday night for real?"

It wasn't like she hadn't endured this kind of abuse

before—*many* times. But at least this once she had a lofty comeback. "I'll have you know that I'm not only going out. I'm going to a bar," she informed him.

"Wow. I'm impressed. Going to drink and carouse and raise hell, huh?"

"I certainly am."

"Especially the drinking, I bet," he said gravely. "If you actually manage to finish a whole beer, make someone take a photograph. I'm almost positive you could sell it to Ripley's Believe It or Not!"

"All right, all right, quit giving me a hard time. Just tell me straight—" She motioned to her black slacks and ruby sweater. "You think I'm dressed okay to go to a bar?"

"I think you could wear that anywhere. You look delectable."

"I don't want to look delectable. And I don't want to do this at all," she grumped. "Miranda and Jane and Kath—you know, the women I work with—they bullied me into this stupid idea. It's Ruben's Bar, you know that little place on the corner of Stark and Walnut? They keep saying it's safe. Just some nice people going there to hear some live music. Only, if it turns out to be a singles' meat market, I'm gonna die."

"I think it's a singles' meat market. Wild and dangerous. I'll bet you have ten guys come on to you in the first hour. It'll be good for you. Get the blood pumping, remind you that every guy isn't Mark."

"I *know* every guy isn't Mark," she said irritably. "That water is two years over the dam."

"Exactly. You've waited forever to get your feet wet again. Where's your courage? Where're your guts?"

Rachel was unsure whether to laugh—or to beat her head against the nearest wall. They'd had conversations like this a zillion times. In fact, Greg's blunt, brotherly teasing about her lack of sex life had always seemed reassuring. Obviously he wouldn't regularly push her to go out with other guys if he had any personal interest in her himself. Their sibling-like sparring relationship had always suited him as perfectly as it suited her.

Only, her feelings had changed, Rachel mused uneasily. Nothing was the same since his accident. She didn't want to embarrass him—or herself—by letting on that she loved him in a different way now. She'd never been tempted to kiss him before. She'd never felt sexual awareness shivering through her nerves when he was in the same room. It was all those evenings in the hospital, alone together, waiting out his stretches of pain, talking about matters of the heart, laughing sometimes, talking about religion and life hurts and dreams. She'd just gotten to know him so deeply, so differently.

But apparently it wasn't that way for him. Especially tonight, it was obvious he thought of her as a sister-pal just like he always had.

"Oh my God," he murmured when he stepped into her living room and saw the generous array of boxes. "Erase the previous question. You've got *plenty* of guts. Is there any clothing store in Milwaukee that still has any stock left?"

"Hey, I only bought what you asked me to. Besides that—give a thief a key to the bank vault, and what do you expect?" With a grin, Rachel curled up in the worn blueberry brocade chair and viewed Greg's horrified face with unrepentant relish.

Normally Stoner made himself thoroughly at home in her living room—which always tickled her funny bone. Greg was the one with the fancy, superduper house, and her place was the rental reject, yet he'd always hung out here. She had nothing worth beans. Thankfully, a few philodendron and ivy and fern plants had had nonstop unprincipled sex over the last couple years, because they managed to fill up the empty corners. She'd found the blueberry and rose print couch at a garage sale—it only sank on one side. Someone in the neighborhood had been throwing out the Duncan Phyfe tables—they'd been resuscitated with stripping and glue and stain. The sound on her TV worked most of the time.

So often Greg had come over—like to fix her shower drain, or to diagnose if she could get a last gasp out of the washing machine—and somehow he always ended up staying. Watching idiot sitcoms on the tube with her. Raiding her fridge for leftovers. Leaving a glove there, a book here, as if he were half living at her place.

But tonight he stood in the middle of the room and scarfed a hand through his hair as if dazed. "Hell, Rach. I never meant for you to go to all this trouble. I know I gave you a list of stuff, but I guess I didn't realize what I was asking. Now I see all these boxes—"

"Don't waste a good guilt attack on me, big guy. You're the only one allergic to shopping in this room. For a long time I thought *sale* and *orgasm* were synonyms. And I just want you to glance at the clothes, okay? You can try the stuff on at home, but let's just make sure you're okay with the styles and colors I picked out."

"I'm sure everything's great. And I really appreciate your doing this."

"Stoner. At least open a box or two. New clothes won't bite you."

"Honest, I was going to look," he assured her.

That was a total lie, Rachel figured, but she still bullied him into opening the packages. For her sake. Not his. As suspected, Greg emerged from each box with a prompt, hearty "Man, this is great. You've got such great taste. I like it a lot, thanks" before hustling to the next box. He didn't really notice a thing—but Rachel could see how the fabrics and colors were going to look on him. His clothes had been pitiful before. Outdated, ill-fitting, ugly. And no, Stoner wasn't destined to become a contemporary Beau Brummel—anything too trendy would probably give him a heart attack. But he had plenty of money, so there was no reason his play clothes had to look like second-hand store rejects when he could afford high retail. And his company favored formal business attire, but even a stereotype, button-down accountant would be ashamed of Greg's suits. Buying new clothes for him had been a downright delirious pleasure. Stoner could have always looked sharper. He just never gave a damn.

And maybe he didn't give a damn now, but her forcing him into looking through the boxes meant he was busy. And his being busy gave her an unobtrusive opportunity to stare at him to her heart's content.

It was just amazing how different he looked.

And how differently he didn't.

He'd never been a bad-looking man, she mused. But the extra weight he'd carried around his middle had always made him look flabby and older. His round-shouldered posture and clothes added to that dorky sort of image. He'd been the kind of guy you could look right at in a crowd and not see. The kind of guy who knew the answers in high school physics but either stumbled or stuttered if he had to talk to a girl. Well, he didn't look like that now.

But the more Rachel studied him, the more she felt stunned by an unexpected realization.

Yeah, he'd lost some weight. And grown some hair.

And the surgeon had done something to make his jaw look more strong and square.

But his eyes and mouth and height and inherent bone structure were exactly the same. The only truly drastic difference was in Greg's attitude, not in his bones. He was walking differently, moving differently—as if he'd been faking that absentminded shuffle all this time. The longer hairstyle wasn't wild or flamboyant, but suddenly he'd lost the bookish appearance. Why, he'd always been gorgeous, she thought. Which made her wonder why on earth he'd gone to so much effort to conceal his natural good looks all these years.

For the immediate present, though, his expression reflected the relief of a true martyr. He'd finally finished opening all the boxes. "Rach, honest, I owe you big. And you're going to be late if I stay any longer—I'll get all this stuff together and get out of your hair. Thanks again for doing the shopping—really thanks—"

An idea had been forming in her mind. Now she said impulsively, "Would you consider going with me?"

Greg was just starting to stockpile boxes in his arms. "Go where?"

"To this bar tonight."

"With you and three other women on a girls' night out? Thanks, but no. I'd rather get hives."

She grinned...but persevered. "They're nice people, honest. Good company. You'd have fun, I promise."

He hesitated. "Did you suddenly get scared about going out? Rach, it's not a predator bar. I was just pulling your chain to tease you. It's no different than the friendly little neighborhood bars all over Milwaukee. Maybe there'll be some singles looking to hit on a Friday night, but basically it's just a low-key place to socialize—people all ages, some playing cards and pool. You'll be fine."

Normally Rachel would have let him be—if he wanted to spend his Friday night alone, it wasn't her business. But as many friends had visited him in the hospital, almost no one had seen him since he got the bandages off, and she knew he was uncomfortable about his new face. Going out would give him a chance to be around people before rejoining the work force on Monday—but in an atmosphere where she could watch out for him.

Still, Rachel knew him—and was positive he'd turn down the idea if she suggested the outing for his sake. No, he had to believe it was for hers. Stoner had a hopeless chivalrous streak. "Well, maybe I would be fine, but Miranda's driving because she's the only one who lives close to me. And if she happens to pick up a guy, then I'd be stranded, no way to get home."

"If that happens, all you have to do is call me."

Since he was turning stubborn, she had to turn sneaky. She pushed a hand through her hair and tried to look anxious. "Greg, I don't even know how to behave in a place like that. I don't know how to *be* single again. The whole thing makes me feel so awkward. Couldn't you come with me just this one time? If I swear never to ask you again?"

He was weakening, she could see. He'd never turned her down when she'd asked for anything yet. Still, he protested one more time. "Rach, you don't need me. You've got a whole female support system, for Pete's sake—"

"That's the point. They're not guys. How many times have you hassled me all these months about turning down dates? And okay, I'm willing to go out. But I just don't feel safe, and that's the truth. I knew the rules when I was a teenager, but it's been that long since I was single. I just feel so nervous. Couldn't you go with me just this once?''

"Come on, Rach. You already set this up to go with friends.''

"But they won't mind your coming. In fact, they'll love you. Please? Didn't I do all this shopping for you? Don't you owe me?''

Four

Rachel scooped up a handful of peanuts, marveling at how fascinating the evening was turning out. She'd never liked bars. Even before being married, she'd never felt comfortable near singles' scenes, and bars were the worst places she could fathom to meet anyone serious.

The irony just tickled her funny bone. She was having a terrific time. It was Greg who was having trouble. And even more ironic, Greg had only come because of her appealing to his chivalrous streak—he'd never desert her if he thought she needed help. Yet who'd a thunk it? It was Stoner who need the protecting.

"Everybody want a second round? I'll spring," Greg offered.

A chorus of female voices echoed the same "Yes, you're an angel, Greg" refrain—which made a ruddy color shoot up his neck. Rachel saw the flush, and then watched him escape their all-female table to wend his way through the crowd toward the bar.

He looked good, she mused. Better than good. He'd changed into some of his new clothes before coming— only because he'd been in ill-fitting sweats before that. And he hadn't chosen anything fancy, just khakis and a black crew neck, but the sweater happened to make his shoulders look ten miles wide and the pants cupped that new, lean, tight little butt of his.

He wasn't halfway to the bar before a female hand reached out from the crowd to pat said-infamously-adorable rump.

When he was two-thirds of the way to the bar, another woman "accidentally" bumped into him and attempted to initiate a conversation.

Once he finally reached the bar, he was sandwiched between two women—both of whom tried to talk him up. Rachel watched him tug at his sweater cuff, shift on his feet, jerk with surprise when yet another strange woman did a wink-and-smile at him.

Although it was obviously a crazy thought, Rachel wasn't positive that he didn't need rescuing. Of course he didn't. Greg was a mature thirty-two-year-old. Responsible. Practical. Principled. He ran the whole financial department for a good-sized company, for Pete's sake, besides which, he wasn't shy around women or anyone else. Naturally, having a brand-new face was an unsettling thing to get used to...but the longer Rachel studied him, the less she noticed any big difference.

Yeah, he was leaner. And yeah, the plastic surgeon had rearranged some details here and there. But Greg was still Greg. His eyes were still a warm summer-lake-blue; his expressions still reflected the character of an intelligent man; he had the same gentle ways and manners around

women he always had. There was no way tons and tons
of females hadn't hit on him long before tonight.

"Hey. Rachel, pay attention!"

Rachel's head swiveled back toward her friends. Jane,
Kath and Miranda had all exuberantly sworn that she'd
love this place, which she figured would never happen.
She couldn't imagine being comfortable in a bar...but
Ruben's was okay. Ruben was a real guy—a big, bald
German man with a roar of a laugh—whose idea of dec-
orating was early-cave. Technically Rachel supposed the
bar was a basement. Go down some witch-black stairs,
open a creaky door, then enter a witch-black room. Eventually one's pupils dilated enough to decipher shapes in
the gloom. The bar counter was a slab of varnished wood,
backdropped by gleaming brass rails and mirrors. Peanut
shells carpeted the floor. Bodies hunched over itty-bitty
tables, crowded so close that fannies bumped into fannies—which no one seemed to mind. Past the bar, past a
hall with bathrooms, was another cavelike room with a
live singing group, but that room was so squish-packed
they couldn't get seats.

Rachel was content enough in the front room. Watching
Greg had more than kept her occupied. But as she should
have suspected, the instant Greg walked out of hearing
range, her friends pounced with questions.

Miranda leapt first. "Where've you been hiding him,
girl? How come you never told us about him before?"

"You mean Greg? But I know I've mentioned him before—"

"You mentioned that he was your next-door neighbor.
You never once hinted that he was adorable." Jane tugged
on a four-inch-long earring. "God, I could just eat him
up."

Kath rolled her eyes. "Come on, you guys, you're being disgusting. He's a true-blue nice guy. You shouldn't be talking about him like he was a sex object.'' She added gravely, ''He's got the sexiest butt I've seen in five years.''

Miranda started giggling first, but the chortles caught on with the other two faster than a contagious rash. Rachel could never figure out how three such serious, responsible women could turn into hopeless gigglers when they got away from work—but that's how they were.

Miranda was a twenty-nine-year-old divorcée who worked in Shipping. She was blond, six foot two, could swear like a sailor and raised cats—six of them at last count. Jane and Kath both worked in Accounting; both were brunettes who eternally battled the bulge and had stopped counting birthdays after thirty-five. Jane was a single mom who'd do anything for her kids, and Kath...well, Kath was the loudest, most irreverent giggler of the group, but her face roadmapped some rough life miles and the others had long sensed that her ex-husband had been an abuser of the worst kind.

Rachel remembered her first day at Rudy's Die Cast. She'd just hired on as a clerk, a job that barely paid minimum wage, but this was right after she'd moved here, right after Mark had taken off with the bimbo. Two years later she had the company's six engineers to boss around, but back then she didn't know or care if she ever got a promotion or was going anywhere. Greg had taken her on as a friend...and then the three women at work had taken her under their wing, dragging her to the movies, coaxing her to contribute to their male-bashing coffee breaks, bullying her into shopping. Those long dark weeks until the divorce was finally over, they'd just been there for her. Not prying. Not pushing. Just being women friends. She thought the world of them...except when they were being nosy.

"Come on, Rach, what's the story on Greg? Was he married before? Why's he single?"

Rachel reached for her glass. When she'd tried to order Perrier, she'd been booed under the table and informed that it was a sacrilege to live in Milwaukee and not love beer. Greg had ordered her something fancy, like a German amber or a Bavarian lager. She couldn't tell the difference between any beer and rat poison, but she nursed a sip now from nerves. "I know Greg wasn't married before, but I really don't know why he's still single. If you're curious, there's nothing to stop you from asking him—"

Miranda hooted. "Like we want to hear *his* answer. We want to hear yours, girl."

"Well, honestly, I don't know. He always just seemed married to his job, which he really likes, and it's not like he isn't busy. He has a ton of friends. Does a weekly Tuesday-night poker game with some guys he went to school with. And he does softball and skiing and sports-type things with the men at his work. And until the accident, he always volunteered one night a week at a gym, working with troubled kids—"

"I don't hear about a female in this social program so far. And he lives in that big old beautiful house next to yours all by himself?"

"He says the house is ridiculously too big for him, too. But it's the family home. I guess his great-gramps built it when he came over from Austria, so the house is like the family roots for all of them. Only, his parents retired to Arizona and an older brother works in Japan—at least for the last few years—so if Greg didn't want to live in the house, it was going to be sold to strangers. Too big or not, he loves the place.''

''You're beginning to make him sound like a saint,'' Jane said disgustedly. ''Responsible, good job, cares about family and kids—for Pete's sake, move this along to more interesting stuff. Like how's he kiss?''

Rachel swiftly chugged another sip of beer. ''Why on earth would you think I'd know?''

''If you don't know, somebody certainly should.'' Kath raised a volunteer hand. ''I could find out and report back. Or do you have dibs on him?''

''I don't have 'dibs' on him,'' Rachel said swiftly. ''But—''

''But what? Is he free or not, girl?''

Rachel knew Kath and the other women well enough to be one hundred percent positive they were just ribbing, trying to get a rise out of her. No different than Greg, they'd been harassing her about her nonexistent sex life for months now. And she'd never had trouble taking a joke and laughing at herself…yet now everything was different. The way she cared about Stoner, thought about Stoner and so unexpectedly ached for Stoner made her feel vulnerable from the inside out.

She must have said something appropriate enough, because Kath chuckled. And then shrieks and yells from the other room aroused the women's curiosity as to what was going on in there. The three women wandered in that direction just as Rachel spotted Greg.

His face was oddly flushed, she thought. He was dodging bodies right and left, coming back to the table carrying the fresh drinks, which he plunked down promptly. And then he sank into the chair next to hers. ''Where's the rest of the team?''

''It sounded like some action was going on in the other

room. They just went in there to take a look. What's wrong?''

''Nothing.'' Greg arranged the glasses for the other three, then peered over the rim of hers. ''Wow. I think we should rename you Guzzling Gussie. Another three hours, you'll probably level another inch, huh?''

''Hey, I've been drinking,'' she said defensively.

''Yeah, like it snows in the Amazon. Are we talking a powder-puff problem here? If you don't want beer, I'll go get you one of those girl drinks with an umbrella and a cherry.''

''Are you trying to call me a sissy, Stoner?'' But she was only vaguely listening to his insults. Something odd was going on with him. He'd not only sat next to her but pushed his stool closer, so his hip was grazing her hip. And then he leaned forward with an elbow on the table so that she had an even closer view of his flushed face and dark snapping eyes. ''Something is definitely bugging you—''

''Yeah, I was calling you a powder puff, and just keep looking at me, okay? That guy at the bar was really giving me the third degree on you.''

''What guy?'' Immediately her gaze darted toward the bar.

''Don't look up, shortie! Just never mind altogether. He's nobody you'd be interested in. That's the point. He looks like trouble, so just act like you're tight with me, so he'll get the picture if he looks this way.''

Stoner's protectiveness was sweet—except that the only person pointedly looking in the direction of their table was noticeably female, not male. And the lady was not only looking, but clearly walking toward them. She was attractive, Rachel mused. A little older than Stoner, with neat, tidy brown hair and subtle makeup and clothes that showed a conservative nature—a crisp pleat in her pants, boots, a V-neck sweater. Temporarily, though, it seemed possible she'd exuberantly indulged in a fair amount of beer, judging from the brick-red cheeks and the glazed eyes. One minute she was weaving toward them, the next she was leaning over the table, offering a direct view of her cleavage to a fast-swallowing Stoner. A quarter and dime suddenly sailed around the table.

"You forgot your change, darling. I told Ruben I'd take it to you." The woman smiled with huge significance at Greg, until those blurry brown eyes suddenly realized that he wasn't alone at the table. "Uh-oh. Are you with her?"

"Actually, I can speak for myself," Rachel said cheerfully. "And yes, he's with me. We're not only a pair—we've been married for nine years and have three children. I've got pictures in my wallet if you'd like to—"

"Um, no." The brunette plastered a hand over the open throat of her sweater and rapidly stood upright.

"Well, thanks so much for bringing his change. That was really nice of you," Rachel called after her, and then murmured teasingly to Greg, "So there was a guy after *me,* huh?"

She was positive Stoner wouldn't mind her chasing off the brunette—the woman was obviously inebriated. But Rachel assumed he'd make a joke out of who was protecting whom, and instead he sounded pretty darn serious. "And there was more than one guy looking at you like trouble, besides. This place is usually okay, but maybe it's the crowd tonight. Noisy, smoky, getting wilder by the minute... You let me know when you want to go home, okay?"

From his tone of voice, Rachel had the impression that he was the one who wanted to get out of here, and her jaw almost dropped in surprise. The bar scene had been a ton more interesting and livable than she'd thought. Maybe she'd rather be home, watching a movie and sipping mulled cider with friends by her own fire, but that was just because she had a fuddy-duddy nature. And the point was, she'd really thought Greg was having a fine evening. Women had been fawning all over him nonstop. Wasn't that every guy's favorite daydream? And if a guy had to test out a new face in public, the females drooling over him had to be mighty reassuring.

But abruptly Rachel realized the obvious. Fun or no fun, Stoner was likely exhausted. He'd only been out of the hospital a week. And being a guy, naturally he couldn't admit to a weakness like being tired.

"I wouldn't mind going home, if it's okay with you," she said meekly.

The way Greg leapt to his feet told Rachel she was right about his wanting to head home. Within minutes, she'd told her friends about leaving and the two of them had exited. The night was as crisp as black toast, the air snapping cold. His sedate Volvo wasn't half as peppy as the little red MG that had been destroyed in the accident, but it was quiet and leather-comfortable and the heater roared warmth in just a few seconds.

The silence of the night folded over her. She caught the gleam of ebony water when they crossed the Milwaukee River, and not long after that they were in neighborhood country. This late, most houses were shut down for the night, but it was still the Halloween season. Witches and ghosts decorated lawns; gruesome-faced pumpkins sat on porch steps. A white satin moon backlit the stark tree branches, and tires hissed on wet leaves.

"Never thought I'd appreciate the smell of snow in the air," Greg remarked, "but I seem to be enjoying the oddest things since getting out of the hospital."

"You went through such a long siege," she said sympathetically, but all she could think was how much she enjoyed being with him. And that wasn't news...except that these unexpected feelings for him kept building. A secret excitement charged the air when they were together, a champagne awareness that made life bubble brighter, a yearning that kept growing instead of going away. She leaned her head against the headrest. "I was afraid you might have overdone, going out tonight."

"No, I couldn't feel better. And you were right about your friends. They were easy to be with. Good people."

"Well, they figured out that you were good people, too. Except for Jane, who works for a comptroller. She had to meet you in person to be absolutely positive you didn't eat chunky redheads for breakfast or what you'd think about being around the riffraff working class."

Greg chuckled. "My dad made a living with his hands. So did my gramps and great-gramps. Take away inflation, and I think they probably made comparatively a better living and wouldn't be too impressed with my fancy master's degree. I don't have much patience with anyone who does the snob thing."

"I know you don't. " She smiled at him, then shifted in her seat. "The whole neighborhood seems to be asleep...except for the light in Mr. Rembrowsky's window."

"I thought he'd still be up." Greg shot her a dry look. "Leo was at his front window when we left the house together earlier. I'd suggest that we strip naked and streak past his house, because it'd give him something fun to talk about? Only, I'd guess he fell asleep in his chair, his binoculars in his lap, trying to wait up for us."

"He does have quite a nosy streak, doesn't he? But I like him."

"So do I. He's a wonderful old guy. And his nosiness seriously does good rather than harm—at least most of the time. He's always watching out for the women in the neighborhood, making sure you're all in when you're supposed to be and safe. Or…"

"Or he calls you?" Rachel guessed wryly. But she forgot the subject of their neighbor when Greg pulled into her driveway instead of his own. "Hey, you didn't have to bother driving me to my door. I could have run across our yards, for heaven's sake."

"Yeah, well, it's past midnight and freezing and I saw that lightweight coat you were wearing."

"This coat's plenty warm," she immediately defended. But the instant they both climbed out of the car, her teeth started chattering and she couldn't help stomping her feet. Naturally he noticed. The car had just been so snuggly warm that the sudden contrast of night air was like a slap of ice. With one of those disgusting all-male grins, Stoner hiked around the car to throw an arm around her shoulder.

"You didn't think to get your house key out, did you, when the car lights were still on?"

"Nope."

"And you didn't think to leave the back porch light on, for safety if not for a little illumination?"

"Nope."

"So I'll try and keep you from freezing to death while you find the key."

That's it. She was going to have to knock his block off for all this teasing, but somehow she couldn't hold on to that nice, safe, righteous mood.

Swiftly she ducked her head, while her fingers dived through her corduroy purse. Greg was just blocking the wind, his arm around her shoulder just offering a little warmth…yet her pulse responded as if someone had injected a dose of joy juice in her veins. Her senses suddenly seized on every detail about him. His navy jacket, his height, the streak of silver moonlight on his cheek, the way his longish hair rifled away from his brow. That fast, her hormones surged awake, cavorting through her nerves, sensitizing her breasts and making her belly tighten. She recognized the thrill of desire. She also recognized she was responding to him like a lovesick teenager suffering a first crush.

Only, she was years away from being a teenager. And she hadn't wanted a man in a blue moon—until this new madness for Greg had shown up. Every time, the desire was stronger. Every time, it shocked her with the punch of power.

Greg was still talking to her, still teasing her about something. She was still trying to find the house key in the purse. Yet her ears drummed such a loud awareness of him that she couldn't think of anything else. *Don't be a damn idiot and do anything,* she warned herself. She'd kissed him in the hospital. If he'd wanted to make anything of that, he could have. He hadn't. And he'd behaved like a big brother with her all evening. In a dozen ways he couldn't have made it more clear that he felt nothing romantic for her. She'd have to be crazy to risk ruining a wonderful friendship by pushing something he obviously didn't want....

"You've still got your screen door on," he remarked.

"Huh?" She raised her head, thinking, How did a screen door get in this conversation? And there were his eyes, dark, sexy, luminous in the darkness, distracting her even more.

"I know it's been a late fall, but we could wake up any morning with three feet of snow on the ground. You haven't got any of your storm windows or doors on. You need some help?"

Help with insanity, maybe. She bent her head again so he couldn't read her expression. Frantically her fingers searched for the house key in her purse. She tried to make her voice sound sensible and normal. "I'll get the windows done. I just couldn't seem to catch a Saturday free earlier—"

"Because you've been helping me."

"Because I'm lazy and hate storm windows with a passion," she corrected him humorously.

"Well, I'll make you a deal. I'll help with your storm windows on Sunday afternoon...if I can get a free dinner out of the deal."

"Stoner, you're still recovering from a broken arm. You don't need to be doing any physical work. And you don't need to bribe me. It's not like you're a hundred percent yet, and you're starting work again. I was already going to make some stuff for your freezer. Sauerbraten, maybe a dinner of schnitzel and spaetzle, maybe a little apple cake. It's not like I don't know your favorites...." Her fingers finally located the metal teeth of the house key and emerged from her purse. She exhibited the key with a triumphant expression...but there were his eyes again, waiting for her, not seeming to look at the key at all but just at her shadowed face.

"I figured you'd find those keys sometime before dawn," he teased.

"Hey, I found them, didn't I? If you're going to give me grief, you can forget it on the apple cake and the sauerbraten—"

"God. I'm sorry. Beyond sorry. I'll never tease you again as long as I liv—"

Don't screw it up, Rachel told herself. *Don't Don't*...Just before she reached up and kissed him.

Oh, man. Oh, man. Heaven knew why she let herself go with the impulse, because her lips barely grazed his before she recognized instantly, painfully, that she was making a total fool of herself. Greg didn't reject her—he didn't have a cruel bone in his body—but he distinctly froze. His eyes opened wide. His shoulders locked still.

She squeezed her eyes closed, wishing there was some nearby quicksand she could bury herself in. Jolting—fast, she backed down on her heels, not looking at him, her mind racing to find some apology or excuse that would make this right. Maybe he'd believe that six sips of beer had made her inebriated?

Yet it seemed Greg only froze for that quarter of a millisecond. Suddenly she felt his fingers sieving through her hair, his palm cupping her head. From nowhere she saw his mouth coming, coming, coming down, homing on her lips the way life sought sunlight.

Her keys fell to the ground, abandoned.

She'd kissed him in the hospital and felt the connection. These days all she had to do was walk in the same room with him to feel the connection. But there'd been no magic before. Stoner had never kissed her back before. She'd sensed the spark, but she'd never seen what flint could do rubbed against a natural hard, hot surface. Emotion poured off Greg like he'd been holding it back for a couple of decades.

A groan emerged from his throat as if it'd been trapped there. On an acid-cold night his mouth touched hers, tasted hers, treasured hers with savoring gentleness. His arms swept around her, slowly, caressing and rubbing as his hands wound around her and then held on.

Fabrics crunched and creased between them—not just

coats, but bulky sweaters—yet Rachel could feel her breasts swelling, burning, responding in the most elemental way to being crushed against his chest, his heat, his thudding heartbeat. He was aroused. She could feel that part of him, too, pressed and pulsing against her abdomen.

She couldn't catch her breath. His kiss deepened, darkened, her lips parting under the pressure of his. Tongues touched tongues—wet, soft, smoking. She tasted hunger in his kiss. She tasted need. She tasted the magic of longing. Longing for him. Just him. Not for sex, not for a man, not for release from the physical pleasure of sensation and frustration. This yearning was solely and only for Greg.

Emotions swirled through her heart with dizzying speed. The way she couldn't catch her breath, she couldn't catch her common sense. This newness seemed impossible. She knew him, trusted him. Yet these moments with him were as if she'd never heard the hush of night, never saw moonlight before, never saw the grass glistening like diamonds on a fall night before. Fear whispered through her. Of course she knew what desire was. Of course she knew what these feelings were. Only, not exactly. She'd never felt excitement like this, rich and raw and explosive. All this time, she'd never doubted the physical relationship with her ex-husband had always been fine...yet now she thought, My God, how could I not have known there was so much more?

"Rach..."

She heard his rough whisper. But his mouth came right back down and took hers again, hard, rough, exhilaratingly.

"Rachel..."

He never used her full name, Rachel, unless he was dead serious, but he'd barely said it before he was kissing her yet again. Her neck ached from the pressure of his kisses; her toes ached from arching to meet his greater height. She didn't care. All this time she hadn't known he wanted her back.

All this time she hadn't known he wanted her at all.

All this time her best friend had kept it secret that between the two of them they had something incredible.

"Rach." His mouth lifted. Fingers brushed the hair from her forehead, dropped to her shoulders, steadied her. She saw his dark eyes through a dream haze. It was hard to think, when that wild, delirious sizzle was still galloping through her bloodstream. "I lost my head."

"And I lost mine." She grinned, likely a goofy grin. But this was Greg. So what if they both lost their minds? What was wrong with that?

But apparently there was something wrong. To him. A frown creased his brow; his eyes darted away from her. He took a short, harsh breath, as if seeking control. Then he bent down to pick up her keys, jerked the house key in the lock and rapidly pushed open her back door.

"I'm sorry, Rach. Really sorry. I know you didn't expect that to happen and neither did I. We'll just forget it, okay? And it's freezing out here—you head in where it's warm. I'll see you tomorrow."

Rachel stepped in, mostly because she felt too bewildered to say anything—at least anything coherent. Within seconds, he'd closed the door and he was striding for his car, and her chance to say anything was gone.

Her heart hadn't stopped galloping that fast. The lush, rich, urgent sensation of desire hadn't disappeared that fast, either. Hurt stabbed, sudden and sharp. That Greg returned her sexual feelings could have been stunningly wonderful…and instead he felt "sorry."

She didn't understand why.

She leaned against the sink, watching his car pull into his driveway, watching him walk to his house, his hair shining in the moonlight. Just the look of him warmed her from the inside out. He loved her. She'd really known that for a long time. She just couldn't fathom why Stoner would think it was seriously bad news for the love of a friend to turn into a different, deeper type of love.

She was the one who'd always had the love allergy. Divorce was so common these days that one would think the experience would be relatively easy. Not for her. For her it was like someone ripped out her heart and hung it naked in public. She never thought she'd get over it. She never thought she'd want to touch another man as long as she lived.

And until Greg's accident, Rachel truly hadn't known that she'd finally healed and moved onto another emotional place. Discovering her new feelings for him was a source of wonder rather than wariness. And yes, of course she had been—and still was—worried about ruining a good friendship. But if Greg felt a matching desire, what was the problem?

Was there a reason she didn't know? Why he didn't or couldn't love her?

Five

On Monday morning, Greg climbed out of his Volvo in the parking lot of Bracken & Worth. As he crossed the street toward his company's front door, he heard a wolf whistle coming from the neighboring construction site. Some knee-jerk response made him glance around.

A champagne blonde in a hard hat and jeans was driving a forklift next door. The instant she caught Greg's eye, she enthusiastically waved and whistled again. Confused, he turned his head to locate the source of her admiration. Seconds later, his face flushed cranberry red.

There was no one else around.

Which seemed to mean that she was whistling at him. *Him.*

Holy moly.

He didn't gallop into the office, because, of course, he was the head of Finance. His job didn't specifically require him to behave with dignity and authority, but running hell-bent for leather lacked a certain decorum. Still, he scraped back his hair the instant he entered the building and hustled toward the elevator.

"Excuse me? Sir?"

An image of Rachel seeped into his mind, no differently than she had a dozen times since Friday night. Technically there was no reason the crazy woman construction worker should have suddenly reminded him of Rachel...yet both invoked a similar problem. Ever since the plastic surgeon removed the bandages from his face, Greg felt like he'd been plunked down in the middle of an alien planet where he didn't know any of the road signs or rules.

"Excuse me! Sir! Sir, you can't go upstairs without authorization—"

No one was treating him the same—and obviously Greg realized that his change in appearance was the reason. But he was still *him*. Still the same old frog. Nothing remotely related to a prince. Yet even women who knew him suddenly seemed to expect him to *be* different. It was the hairiest, eeriest thing he'd ever experienced. And people like the construction woman were strangers and didn't matter, but Rachel...

Rachel mattered badly to him.

And he'd about die before hurting her.

"Sir!"

Stubby fingernails suddenly clutched the arm of his suit jacket. Greg halted in surprise. And then, eyebrows still raised, he automatically smiled at Bracken & Worth's receptionist. The plump brunette manning the front desk had always been a cheerful, responsible sort. "Good morning, Brenda. I meant to say hello when I walked in, but temporarily I was distracted—" Abruptly he hesitated. "You were calling out for *me?*"

"Yes, sir." Now it was her turn to frown and hesitate. "I'll be darned. Mr. Stoner?"

"Yes, of course…" And then he sighed. Did every female acquaintance have to respond to him with that same look of shock? "I can see you had trouble recognizing me. I'm afraid I had several surgeries following the car accident—"

"Yes, sir, I know. We all know. And I knew you were coming back to work today, too. I just… You look so completely different. You look…wonderful, Mr. Stoner. Just wonderful. Just fabulous. Just—"

Nervously Greg tugged hard on his tie and skedaddled upstairs as soon as he could. Still, he got the same kind of mortifying greeting from Linda in Human Resources, then Madge and Opal in the data processing pool. There was no chance of relaxing until he reached his multiroom accounting department.

Thankfully this was still his work home. Nothing had dared significantly change in his two-month absence. Greg hiked through the main room, calling greetings to each of his eight-person staff, feeling his nerves start to ease.

In the financial world, certain things were as predictable as the sunrise. Come hell or high water, payroll had to get out—and there was always a problem with payroll. Come hell or high water, taxes had to be paid—and there was always a problem with taxes. The walls were a nice, soothing gray, the carpet a nice, soothing tweed. And his accounting staff never registered that he looked any different, because they wouldn't. They were wonderful. They would never remark on anything personal. His staff could be counted on for certain predictable things. They lived for budget crisis. They watched *Jeopardy* and lied about their scores. And they'd grown up wanting to color between the lines.

Past the long main room was his office—which was even more of comfort zone. The vault was in his office. His seven-button phone. His customized keyboard and a skinny-window view of the Milwaukee River. Greg sank into his familiar teal leather desk chair. Within minutes, his desk was neatly heaped with crisis-level problems of petrifying priorities, and his staff helpfully trotted through the door with more.

He made it through two contented hours of nonstop work before his gaze accidentally tiptoed over to the window. Nothing about the river view reminded him of Rachel. Yet faster than a gunshot, there she was again, shooting through his mind as if she'd just been prowling around waiting for any old trigger.

Their embrace Friday night played through his memory in intricate detail. The texture of her silk-soft lips. The shimmery gold strands of her hair in the moonlight. The sough of her breath, honey sweet, as she returned the pressure of his kisses and invited more.

Greg didn't get it. Then or now. How a woman could have been married all those years—even if it was to El Creepo Sacred Mark—and still kiss like an innocent, joyful girl. Happy. That's how she kissed. As if she were happy to be with him, thrilled to be touched by him, heart-skidding, giddy-high, joyfully happy to drive a guy clear out of his mind.

And all this time he'd been successfully crystal-careful around her. She'd aroused him before—he'd been harder than a steel girder around her before—yet he'd still managed to keep a lid on his hormones. A grown man did what a grown man was supposed to do. He'd steered clear because there were differences between them. Not paltry differences like class or race or religion. Their differences were way more serious.

He was a nerd. She was sunlight. He had a staid, practical nature. She was excitement from her toes to her blond crown. Years ago Greg had faced reality: he was boring to most women. Hell, he even bored himself in the relationships he'd tried, and God knew sex was never like a romance novel for him. Worth doing, yes. Worth destroying his life for, no. And as a friend, that sort of thing didn't matter so much. But as a lover, Greg was unwilling to risk failing Rachel. He admitted his reasons were selfish.

It would destroy him to fail her.

He wandered over to the window, staring out, jingling the change in his pocket. All that emotional junk was old news to his heart and conscience. But somehow he'd forgotten it all last Friday night.

Basically he understood why Rach had come on to him. This had been building. Only a stupid man could have missed the different way she'd been looking at him, the different way she'd been touching him. But Greg knew that wasn't the whole picture.

Right after her jerkwater ex took off with another woman, Rachel had felt like a failure, totally lost faith in her own judgment. For two long years, she'd turned down all dates, never even looked at a guy. But sooner or later those wounds had to heal. Sooner or later she was going to notice that sleeping alone was no fun. Possibly her gaze had suddenly landed on him because he'd had such a startling change in appearance—but Rach didn't love him. She wasn't even necessarily attracted to him. What she felt for him positively, though, was trust.

No true friend would break that trust. Ever. And yes, of course, he'd physically responded to her. She was so beautiful and vital and wonderful that it'd take a saint not to respond—so in itself, responding to her was forgivable.

Maybe even a seriously good thing to do. This was the first time Rach had poked her toe in the life lake since the divorce. She needed a boost in the feminine ego, not a rejection.

He didn't want to reject her. He didn't want her to ever feel that she couldn't trust him. He was just afraid that his suddenly looking different may have confused her, that's all. And the whole problem would surely disappear if he could think of something—anything—that would just put their friendship back on the footing it'd been before.

Only, *what?*

"Greg!"

He quickly pivoted away from the window at the familiar sound of his boss's voice. Monica Kaufman, the CEO of Bracken & Worth, had visited him twice in the hospital. Behind her back, the guy executives called her a ball-breaker, but Greg never had a problem. The men who aroused her bitchy side tended to threaten her. It was easier for him. He wasn't the kind of man who threatened anyone.

She strode in, her mahogany hair swinging, her smile shaped by plum lipstick, her hands outstretched to greet him. Typically she looked the dynamic fifty-two-year-old woman she was. The makeup was flawless, the perfume subtle but meant for a man to remember. The flash of gold at her throat was never ostentatious, always enough to make your eyes shift to there. Her business suits were never so short as to be overtly sexy, but always short enough to make a guy's eyes flicker in the direction of her legs.

Her gaze lapped him in, head to toe. "I was tied up this morning or I would have been in earlier! My God, you look marvelous. More than marvelous. I wouldn't know it was you! And it's wonderful to have you back! You can't imagine how much we all missed you!''

Heels clicking, she descended for a hug—as if they hugged every day. Since they'd never exchanged so much as an air kiss before, Greg automatically had his hands extended for the friendly handshake he assumed was coming. Maybe he swiftly, awkwardly dropped his hand, but it wasn't like it mattered. They'd always gotten along well. He thought the hug was nice of her, really.

Until he felt that long, pampered hand slide down his spine and squeeze his butt.

Holy moly.

Holy cow.

Holy smokes.

He hoped to God he was mistaken, but Greg had a terrible feeling his boss had just made a pass at him.

Before he had a chance to speak, much less exhale an appalled breath, a wild thought pounced in his mind. An ironic thought. Perhaps he was grasping at straws in a desperately mortifying situation, but maybe—just maybe—Monica creating this problem could help him solve the problem with Rachel.

And Greg was willing to do about anything to solve the problem with Rach.

Okay, so it was going to be one of Those Nights, Rachel thought darkly. Her old-fashioned *Apfelkuchen* was fresh out of the oven, still steaming and smelling like heaven. Typically, though, the cake batter had mysteriously dribbled all over her jeans and white mandarin-collar shirt—not counting the generous splotches on the floor. She'd chosen Wednesday night to make the recipe, because who ever interrupted her on a Wednesday night?

But she'd just mixed the apricot jam with the boiling

gelatin—the basis for the *Apfelkuchen*'s glaze—when simultaneously the phone rang and someone knocked on
her back door. She wasn't cleaned up from the first mess.
Her feet were bare, her hair a mess, her hands all sticky
as she grabbed the wall phone, wedged it between her ear
and shoulder and said hello. She listened a moment.
"Mom! I'm glad to finally catch up with you. For a couple days there I thought we were going to end up playing
phone tag with our answering machines all week. Anything new with you or Dad?"

Naturally she burned her finger on the glaze...but that
was because she realized it was Greg rapping on her win-
dowed door. She yelled at him to come in.

Her mom immediately questioned, "Who's that?"

"Sam, my new lover," she said promptly, and once
Greg stomped in, she held the phone in the air and in-
structed, "Sam! Say hi to my mom!"

Greg knew his lines. He yelled out, "Hi, Rachel's
mom. This is Sam, and just so you know I'm an honest
kind of guy—I have no honorable intentions toward your
daughter whatsoever and am leading her down the path
of sin as fast as I can."

Rachel clapped the phone back to her ear. "See,
Mom?"

"That's funny. His voice sounded just like Greg, your
next-door neighbor," her mother said dryly.

"What? You don't trust your own daughter?" She batted at Greg's hands—because he was already trying to
steal a wedge of her apple cake. Unrepentant, he peeled
off his coat, opened the fridge as if he owned the place
and brought out a fresh quart of milk. She snapped her
fingers and motioned toward the cupboard. "Use a glass,
you uncivilized cretin!"

"Excuse me?"

"I wasn't talking to you, Mom. I was talking to my decadent new lover." She continued to carry on conversations with both of them, hamming up the role of Greg as her lover—which eventually invoked a huge belly laugh from her mom. Normally she'd have laughed, too. The conversation was as familiar as sunshine to all three players, and Greg was a terrific sport in his acting role. But it was different for her today, Rachel realized.

Different because she didn't want to be pretending that Greg was her lover. Different because last Friday night's embraces had hung in her mind like moss on an oak tree, swaying and whispering with every sneaky breeze. They'd talked at least a half dozen time since then, but he hadn't said one word. Not about kisses. Not about that embrace. Not about anything that a brother wouldn't naturally say to a sister.

Rachel had been trying to convince herself that his silence was good news. At least he didn't seem to realize she was in love with him. He'd shaken her timbers. But if she hadn't shaken his...well, the one mistake she couldn't survive a second time was the humiliation of believing someone loved her who didn't give a damn.

Finally she hung up from talking with her mother. By then, she'd finished brushing the apricot glaze on the apple cake, and Greg had leveled two glasses of milk and scouted out two plates, two forks and a spatula.

"It's still way too hot to eat," she told him. "Besides, once it's cool, it's supposed to be served with whipped cream. Trust me, it's worth waiting for."

"My theory is, we could willingly burn our tongues on one piece now, and have the second piece with the whipped cream later."

She rolled her eyes. "Is that why you came over? Because you were starving and no one ever feeds you?"

"Yeah. But it isn't the only reason." He shook his head at the state of her kitchen. "Man, do you make a big mess." He started carting over bowls and spoons to the sink, while she squirted in soap and flipped on the hot water. "You know, I don't think most moms hope and pray their single daughters are sleeping around."

"Well, you've met my mom. It's not really orgies on her mind. It's Mark. She thinks he really messed me up, scarred me for life and all that yadda yadda. She's convinced if I just had one serious, juicy affair—even if it didn't lead to marriage—it'd be a sign that I'd healed, moved on, am finally having some real fun and all that nonsense."

He reached for the dishcloth, and instead of applying it to a bowl, swiped her cheek. His touch could have been sensual. Sexual. Evocative. Instead he scrubbed the batter off her cheek and jaw like she was a kid. "I also got the impression that your mom also asks you the same money questions about every time you talk."

"Yes. And so does my dad." She removed the dishcloth from his hand and draped it over his head. But then she sighed. "My parents really wanted to help me financially with the divorce. And maybe I should have let them. I know they worried."

"I can't imagine why. You moved away from Madison and everything familiar two years ago, had no job, no plans, no place to stay, no knowledge of Milwaukee—"

"Hey, whose side are you on?"

"Yours. But you know as well as I do that was a ditz move. No wonder your family was worried."

Rachel told herself that she could surely fall out of love with him. Stoner could be extremely aggravating. Particularly when he got the stupid idea she wanted to hear the truth. "Okay, I've admitted before, moving here was a little impulsive," she said irritably. "But I told you how it was. My parents are wonderful. No mom and dad could ever have done more for me, and still I screwed up. They told me from the beginning that Mark was a taker and a user. I didn't want to hear. And when Mark proved what a dog he was, I had to move away—or I'd have heard a constant stream of I told you so's—and worse yet, they'd have known how badly I was struggling financially. *I* made the mistake, Stoner. I didn't want them to pay for it. Now quit picking on me—"

"I wasn't picking on you."

"—and tell me why you came over."

Greg started cutting the cake. "To talk about sex."

"Sex." Rachel blinked. That particular subject had dominated her mind for days. Sex. With him. Making love. With him. She'd speculated, maybe forty seven times now, if they'd started those kisses last Friday inside the house, where it was more private and warmer and way, way, easier to peel off clothes, if they might have ended upstairs in her bedroom with the lights turned off.

Greg, however, seemed to be absconding toward the living room with two pieces of her cake. At least he'd included one for her, but his attitude implied nothing serious could possibly be on his mind. "Yup. I've got a problem. I'd appreciate your advice."

"Uh-huh. I believe you need my advice about sex like cats fly."

"I'm serious."

"Okay, okay. I'm listening." But her tone was still dubious.

"My boss made a pass."

Rachel stopped dead in the doorway. "Monica? You're kidding me!"

"I only wish." Greg set the two plates on the coffee

table, then stalked over to her fireplace and hunched down to lay a fire. For a man who'd begged nonstop to steal some cake, he seemed to have forgotten about it.

Rachel punched off the TV and turned on a lamp, studying him. His turning into an adorable hunk had certain disadvantages. Two months ago she would have known how to read his expression. Now she could see the grooved frown on his brow, the frustration in those deep blue eyes, but how deeply this problem bothered him wasn't so clear. "Exactly what did she do?"

"Well...on Monday, she came in to say hi, welcome back. Only, she gave me a hug that ended up with her hand on my butt." Greg piled logs on the grate, then stacked kindling, then lurched to his feet. The same way he'd forgotten the cake, he now seemed to instantly forget the fire.

"You couldn't have misunderstood what your boss intended—"

"That's what I thought. Or hoped." Greg rubbed a hand at his nape. "Except that was just Monday. Yesterday she was mostly out of the office, but today, it was one thing after another. She passed me in the hall twice, squeezed my butt both times. Patted down my tie. Asked me out for drinks at the end of the day."

"Eek," Rachel murmured.

"My opinion exactly." He paced around like a cougar in a cage. "I'm thinking of going back to the plastic surgeon and asking for my old face back."

"Stoner, come on, you look wonderful!"

"Wonderful or ugly isn't the point. The point is that people—especially women—are treating me differently because I look different. A woman construction worker whistled at me the other morning. Cracked me up. The receptionist didn't even know who I was. That was a little funny, too. But Monica—there is *nothing* funny about my boss pulling this nonsense.''

''I realize,'' she said sympathetically.

''Rach, I love my job. Really love it. I happen to be damn good at what I do. And I know the whole tango women are supposed to go through with sexual harassment problems—try talking to the supervisor first. Then do a written complaint. Then go over the supervisor's head, press charges. Only, I don't want to do any of that dance. I just don't want it to happen again. I *don't* want to risk losing a job I'm nuts about.''

Rach said quietly, ''You know, if it does come down to quitting, it won't kill you. Another company would snap you up, Greg. You've mentioned several offers you've had even over the last six months—''

''Maybe so. But if I quit, there'd be questions raised about why I left this job. They'd justifiably go after a reference from Monica, and I'd be dead. Of if I tried telling the truth, said I quit because I couldn't handle a woman's attention, to any man in the universe I'd come across as a jerk. Which maybe I am. But—''

''Hey, you. Cut that out. You're not a jerk.''

''Actually, I am,'' Greg said dryly. ''I like women. I get along fine with women. But in romantic relationships, I'm a phhfft. And that's always been my reality.''

''Stoner, it takes two to make any kind of relationship. You're blaming yourself. That's not fair.''

''I'm trying to be honest and realistic about who I am. And apparently my new face is leading certain female people into thinking I'm someone different. Only, I'm exactly the same person. A change in looks doesn't suddenly make me a stud. Or cool. I bored Monica with no trouble before my face surgery. She thought of me as a dependable nerd. A numbers cruncher. A guy who got mustard on his tie. Nobody she thought twice about chasing around the damn office.''

Rachel wanted to respond, but her heart was selfishly pounding, pounding. She couldn't help but think something strange was going on here. He'd asked for her advice. She was glad to give it. But his claiming to be a phhft in romantic relationships seemed pointed. She didn't doubt his problem with Monica, but it just didn't "feel" accidental that he was bringing this problem to her.

She thought he was trying to tell her to forget that kiss, forget those embraces. Not because he was a "phhhft" in relationships, but because he didn't want to be involved with her that way.

"Anyway…" Greg sank in one of the easy chairs, then hunched forward with his hands on his knees. "I figure you must have had a million guys try patting your fanny, so you'd have some ideas what I should do."

"I married Mark. You think I'm smart?"

"You divorced Mark. I think you're brilliant."

She hesitated, and then told herself to forget her personal feelings and concentrate on the problem he was here for. "Well…I guess this isn't very ethical. But when I've had someone at work come on to me, I just plain fibbed, said I was already involved with someone else. In principle, I'd rather be honest. But in reality, sometimes a fib saves hurting the other person's feelings and cuts off any more trouble at the pass."

"I'm not proud. I don't mind lying. But if I suddenly mention to Monica that there's a woman in my life—right after she's made these overtures—she's going to smell it for the lie it is."

She thought, then said slowly, "I see what you mean. But what if I pick you up for lunch at work tomorrow…or come have lunch with you at work?"

"You mean, you're offering to fake being my significant other?"

"Why not? I think you're right—she'll suspect you're lying if you suddenly mention a woman. But if others in the office *see* you with a woman, it's got a chance to come off more naturally. And what have you got to lose? We could at least try it—particularly before she's had a chance to try any more passes."

"Aw, hell. I don't know. I wanted some advice, but I didn't mean to drag you into this—"

"You're not dragging me into anything. We'll have a great time. Don't we always? It's just me you're playing with, remember? And when I pick you up at lunch tomorrow, I'll give you a fast course in sending keep-off signals."

"Keep-off signals?" He looked blank.

She nodded. "You send out friendly body language, Greg—because you like people, and being friendly just comes natural. But the reality is that you *do* look different now. And maybe some women could get the impression that those same friendly signals mean something different—like that you're trying to tell them you're available."

"No way. Honestly, Rach. It's not that I'm above that kind of game playing. It's that I never understood women well enough to even pretend to play that way—"

"Stoner, I realize you didn't intentionally do anything. Obviously. Or you wouldn't be so miserable. But if we just practice some role playing, I can show you what kind of signals we women tend to read," she said cheerfully. "Like…I'll play the manipulative vamp, the lonely crush, the single manhunter. And you can try responding. We'll work on it."

Ten minutes later she ushered him out the back door, his arms laden with half her *Apfelkuchen*. She got a kiss for a thank-you. A swift, brotherly smack on the cheek, wrapped with a grin...but for one stark second, his gaze glued on her face, studying her with such a raw, yearning look of hunger that her pulse soared like a swan in flight. Then he was gone.

She folded her arms, watching him hike across the yard, conscious that she was tapping her foot impatiently on her kitchen linoleum. Maybe she was nuts. Maybe she was dreaming it. But it *seemed* like he kissed her, touched her, looked at her as if she were far more precious than a female friend. And their whole conversation had put a nagging thought in Rachel's head that refused to disappear.

Stoner didn't see himself as a lover. For some goofy reason, he seemed to see himself as a nerd. A phffft in the relationship department. A frog instead of a prince.

Still frowning, she locked the back door and yanked off the light. Until the plastic surgery, Greg's self put-downs always seemed humorous—or intended that way. That he could seriously lack confidence in himself as a man seemed impossible. She climbed the stairs for bed, considering what she wanted and needed to do about their lunch together tomorrow. When she'd proposed the idea, it seemed a way to help him.

Now it seemed like a test. A line in the sand. For her— and for both of them.

Six

Greg punched in a series of numbers, then watched the computer spit out an appallingly large total. His long medical leave of absence had at least one tremendous plus side. He definitely felt needed.

Advertising had gone over budget. Human Resources were screaming they needed two additional staff that no funding had been planned for. It had always been Greg's job to squeeze more blood from the turnip when everyone else had given up and claimed there was no way.

He'd find a way. Impossible financial problems were his favorite kind.

Something fuzzy and black wandered into his peripheral vision, which he ignored. He was capable of ignoring a tornado—and had—when he was concentrating hard.

A heavy object was plunked on his office couch, then something lighter whooshed to his tweed carpet. His brain registered that the offending person causing these interruptions appeared to be settling in instead of leaving, but he never looked up. "Be with you in a minute. Just hold on," he barked, and continued punching numbers.

A throaty chuckle whispered in the air. A sultry feminine perfume attacked his nostrils. "Being dedicated is so like you, darling."

He didn't recognize the sexy chuckle or the frightening perfume. Didn't care. But the "darling" made his head shoot up in confusion. No one called him darling. Ever. As far as he knew, no woman had called a man that corny endearment outside of the movies in four decades.

He intended to make eye-to-eye contact with the interloper, but some male primal instinct took over and his gaze never made it as high as his visitor's face. There were breasts, and then there were breasts. No man who was still breathing could ignore these. Nothing about them *exactly* broke the law. The V neck of a soft angora black sweater showed enough cleavage to make a man sweat, but nothing described in the decency laws—alas—was exposed. It was just that these particular breasts happened to be full and firm and ripe and clearly unencumbered by a bra—or anything else—beneath that sweater.

Being a mature, grown-up male adult, naturally he noticed other things. It was snowing. Well, he hadn't looked, but hell, it was November in Milwaukee. If it wasn't snowing, the odds were it would any second, so that was a safe bet. As far as anything else happening outside, who cared anyway?

The owner of the breasts suddenly kicked off a pair of high-heeled black shoes. Slim legs danced toward him, caressed only by silk stockings, the view unfairly obscured by a skirt that swirled around her knees. The lethal perfume danced closer. Then pounced.

A hundred and ten pounds suddenly hurled—and

curled—in his lap. It was enough to take a guy's breath. Not her weight. But feeling the smooth, warm intimate curve of her fanny nestled right over his zipper. Red fingertips tiptoed up his chest, then climbed around his neck. "How's my sweetie pie today? How's my poochkin? I brought a picnic basket for lunch, but knowing you, darling, I thought you might be hungry for a little appetizer first."

Lips hovered that looked painted with liquid berries, then nailed his mouth with sweet, soft, lethal pressure.

Okay, he thought. *Okay. I'm not going to have a heart attack. I just need a second to get a grip.*

Even hit with a stun gun, his mind continued to function at a certain logical level. Rach never wore her hair in all those frothy curls. She never wore that exotic kind of perfume. And a strange panicked alarm affected his pulse to think she'd actually gone to work that morning without a bra—particularly when she worked with *way* too many men—but that wasn't the point.

The point, Greg logically determined, was that she was obviously playing the game. Just like she said she would. For a second there—a stroke-threatening second—he'd just forgotten her promise to show up for lunch and make out like they were A Pair. In addition, he considered judiciously that her hurling herself in his lap like a wanton, brazen vamp was actually brilliant evidence that their conversation the night before had gone well. Rach was really hamming up her part with wicked exuberance. It just had to be The Game—which meant she'd understood his careful conversation last night about still being the same old nerdy Greg no matter what his appearance looked like now.

So everything was cool. Except for his thundering heart trying to explode in his chest. He thought, I don't feel like a nerd when I'm with her. I feel like a red-hot knight who could rescue her from dragons. He thought, I have to get a grasp on reality. That's all. Even part of a grasp. Even a teensy bit of a grasp.

Only, she kept kissing him, and beneath the berries and the perfume and the sexy look was still Rach. She still tasted like Rachel. She still lured him like Rachel. He moved in to the kiss, in to her. His pulse dipped and his hormones did a free fall from a jet's height, spinning, spiraling, swirling light and heat all through him. Her light. Her heat.

Her breasts crushed against his chest, and somehow his hand was stroking, stroking. Sieving through her hair, whispering down her neck, teasing and caressing down her shoulder, her side. She groaned against his lips, hauling in a lung full of air, then coming back for another kiss…and another and another.

His rotten, annoying conscience tried to insinuate caution, reminding him again that she'd been celibate since the breakup with Sacred Mark. She'd penned up desires for a long time. And he looked different. And this dumb game they'd thought up may have loosened some inhibitions, because she believed he was safe and trustworthy. None of this necessarily meant she felt anything seriously for him.

Greg heard the mental voice of his conscience—and snapped off the volume. He didn't want caution, didn't want to think, and for damn sure, didn't want her to stop kissing him. He wanted exactly what he had—this crash of need, this hot slug of desire. With her, nothing had ever been tepid. It'd always been a hurricane, not just a storm. A thousand fireworks, not just a candle. And she was the power source for all that vital vibrancy, all that life and emotion and zest. It wasn't him. It had never been him. But when he was with her, what he felt with her always expanded his heart beyond his world's horizons.

She shifted, trying to curl closer, still kissing him, still making his blood pound. His fingertips brushed against her breast, and then the heart of his hand strayed, cupping her, feeling the plump flesh heat and firm for him. He wanted to touch her directly, not through the damn sweater. Her weight crushed a nerve in his thigh. He didn't care. His shoulders knotted with tension. He didn't care. He was so hard and cramped that his future children could be jeopardized. He didn't care about anything— except getting Rachel alone, where he could peel up that angora sweater and peel down her stockings and...

"Greg, I wondered if you might—oh! Oh. I apologize. I assumed you were alone—"

He heard his boss's voice...but it was like noticing a bruise in the middle of a train wreck. He was the train wreck. Monica showing up was just a nuisance compared to the problem that mattered.

Rach, though, instantly stiffened. Her head whipped around. Her stocking feet slammed to the floor. An elbow jabbed his ribs as she pushed off his lap and stood up.

She seemed to be recovering a ton faster than he was. Worse yet, he had no interest in recovering...but obviously he had to make an effort. "Monica, this is a close friend of mine, Rachel Martin. And—"

Rach swung around his desk with her hand extended, saving him from having to finish the introductions. "Greg's mentioned you so many times. I'm so glad to meet you. I'm just so embarrassed. When I walked through the outer offices, there was no one here, so I just assumed the whole staff was at lunch—"

Monica's handshake looked as stiff as a fire poker. "There's no problem. It's the noon hour. And as you already pointed out, the offices are temporarily deserted—'' she cocked her head "—Rachel, did you say your name was?''

"Yes. Although I'm not surprised you've never heard of me. Greg's always had the habit of calling me by nicknames, haven't you, sweetie? And listen, if you two have business together, I'll just step outside. I don't want to be in your way—''

"No, no, that's not necessary.'' Monica's gaze swiftly took in the picnic basket on the couch, Rachel's glowing eyes—and stockinged feet. "I had no reason to expect Greg was even here. All I wanted was to ask him a question—which will easily wait until later this afternoon. Have a nice lunch.''

"Why, thanks. We will.''

Even after Monica left, Rachel stood there for a minute with her back turned, staring after his boss. "Whew. She's a high-potency package, isn't she? No wonder you were freaked when she came on to you.''

Greg's mind was as organized as a cyclone. And maybe Rach's voice and sense of humor sounded like normal, but his eyes were still glued to that low-cut black sweater and the silky long legs and the whole sensual hair and makeup. "Um…you're more than a high-potency package yourself, Rach. Did you actually dress like that for work?''

She turned around with a grin. "The sweater and skirt, yes. But I tried to think how I'd modify the outfit if I were really meeting a lover for lunch. My bra's in my purse. I carried the high heels. I added some makeup and the hotsy-totsy perfume. And come on…wait until you see what I brought for lunch.''

"Lunch,'' he echoed, but he was thinking about Rach meeting a real lover, not a pretend lover. Brazenly, playfully seducing the guy she loved, not just a pretend guy. How she'd feel free to play—to be wanton and wild and naturally sensual—with the right man. Not the pretend man.

"Lunch," she repeated, and motioned him over to the carpet in front of his desk. From the couch she opened her picnic basket, and unfurled a blanket to sit on as if this were a real picnic. Then she crouched down and started setting out dishes. "Just for the record, these are all aphrodisiac foods. Lover foods."

"Aphrodisiac—"

"Uh-huh. I never dreamed we'd be so lucky as to run into Monica right off the bat, but I did think sooner or later someone in the office was bound to walk by. Naturally I kissed you hello—we're supposed to be lovers, for heaven's sake. But after that, if and when someone caught us eating, I figured the type of foods—or the look of our picnic—could help make it appear as if we were unquestionably close. Not just pals, but definitely a physically tight pair."

"Aphrodisiac—" He didn't mean to keep repeating the word, but the goodies emerging from her picnic basket were difficult for a responsible, number-crunching nerd to take in.

"You're hungry, huh?" Her smile never let on that his jaw was gaping open. "Well, naturally, most of these are finger foods. Better to feed each other, yes? And to start with, we have asparagus-prosciutto rolls. Traditionally the French lovers used to eat three courses of asparagus the night before the wedding, for the obvious purpose of, um…"

"I believe I can fill in that blank."

"So try one," she said blithely. "And then there's Parmesan cheese oysters. I cooked these ahead at work, because there's an oven in our lunchroom, and I've just never had them any other way but cooked. Really, though, they're supposed to be eaten raw for full aphrodisiac value. Then you're supposed to gum them a little, take your time savoring the taste, and then the process of sucking the oysters down is supposed to be very orally stimulating.... What's wrong?''

"Nothing. Just a little cough."

"You don't like the oysters?"

"Believe me. I like them. I like them."

"All right. Then we have our basic grapes rolled in almonds and ginger. Grapes, of course, are preferably fed to one another from a prone position. And there's a little strawberry-avocado salad. In Aztec culture, the virginal maidens were locked in their homes when the time came for the avocado harvest. They really were forbidden fruit. The guys called avocados *ahuacatl,* meaning testicles, and the fruit was considered such a powerful sexual stimulant that—''

"I get the picture."

"Definitely a dangerous food for lovers," Rach said gravely. "And to top it off, I brought some Black Russian cake and some honey-almond delight. In India, honey used to be a traditional gift for the bridegroom—so he could keep going and going like the battery. And even way before that, Hippocrates used to prescribe honey for sexual virility. And did you know that Attila the Hun drank himself to death with honey on his wedding night? Which may be why they called it *honey*moon. Anyway, all that's great, but I brought the cake, too, because it's got chocolate and cherries, and both those have an unbeatable aphrodisiac history—''

She was having an awful lot of fun making him flush— from shock at this stuff coming out of Rachel. Not because *he* was shy. But Greg figured he'd better infuse a little hormone killer into this conversation before he waded into further trouble. "You couldn't possibly have done all this incredible research last night...so who'd you uncover all this stuff for? Mark?"

Rachel shook her head. "No...this wasn't the kind of thing he'd get a kick out of. He'd be embarrassed."

Greg said immediately, "Not me."

Another cheeky grin...as she popped a glazed grape between his lips. "I knew you wouldn't be. I could always talk about anything with you. And you know I like to cook—at least sometimes. So this stuff was just fun to research. And I thought it'd give you more things to say to Monica or whoever was around here—you know, more evidence that you have a hot and heavy thing going with someone. Namely me."

He tasted the grapes—which he didn't want. Strawberries and asparagus used to be favorite foods, but he didn't want the fancy rolls or the salad either. And sampling the oysters was out of the question. Because he was sitting on the carpet, he could arrange a position where his suit jacket and bent leg completely hid his erection, but that wasn't the same thing as solving his problem.

The more she talked about aphrodisiacs, the more he thought she was one. Skip the food. He wanted to taste Rachel. Sample her from head to toe. Completely. Thoroughly. Her mouth, her slim white hands, her shapely legs and luscious neck, the lobe of her ear—every inch of her. And the thought of another man trying out even the smallest bite and discovering those same aphrodisiac qualities made him feel downright ill.

But this was, of course, a game to her. A game they were supposed to be sharing and having fun with. A friend helping out another friend.

"You *have* to have a piece of Black Russian cake," she informed him.

"It looks incredible," he complimented her. "But I'm thinking I'd like to cut a piece and save it for my afternoon break."

"Stoner, you're hardly eating." Her face suddenly fell. "Oh dear, don't tell me you don't like—?"

"I love. Everything," he assured her rapidly. Hell. He'd have to kill himself if he hurt her feelings. "It's just this situation with Monica has twisted my stomach in knots. Everything you made is so incredibly delicious that it's killing me not to do justice to it. I just want to save some for later, when I can get the boss off my mind."

Rachel immediately hunched up on her knees, her expression turning serious. "All right. We need to talk about that. About why Monica—and other women—are suddenly coming on to you. And how possibly you've been asking for it."

"Asking for it? Come on, Rach. You know me better than that. I never in a thousand years wanted a problem with my boss like this. For that matter, I never had any kind of problem with Monica—until I got a new nose and a new jaw."

"You turned into a breathtaking hunk," Rachel agreed, with humor in her smile even though her eyes reflected total seriousness. "But—in my opinion—that has little to do with whether a woman looks at a man and sees him as a potential love interest. Or sex interest, for that matter."

"What, you're saying that looks don't matter?"

Rachel sighed. "Yeah, looks matter. We all know that. But I think whether anyone is really handsome or really ugly isn't the point—the point is that *how* we look sends out messages to other people. Are we going to get along?

Is this someone I can talk to? Is this someone I should be afraid of? That kind of thing.''

"Okay, right, I get you now. Go on.''

"So what I'm saying is that if a woman whistles at you—or suddenly sees you as a potential lover—it's not because you have a new nose. It's because you're sending out messages, in the way you walk, the way you move.'' She hesitated, her eyes on his face. "Stoner, you have a long habit of calling yourself a nerd. You almost always say it with a grin, like a joke. And it's an endearing quality, that you can laugh at yourself, come across as natural, human, someone anyone could talk to. But would you find it so hard to believe that other people may never have seen you as a nerd? Especially women?''

He frowned, watching her pack the leftover dishes back in the picnic basket as she talked. "I never thought one way or another about how anybody saw me.''

"Typical male,'' she said wryly. "But what I'm trying to suggest is that the way you walk, the way you move, tells other people that you *like* who you are. That you like being a man. That you enjoy your sexuality. And that's very appealing to a woman—you're not getting me at all, are you?''

He was trying to, since Rachel seemed to be concentrating so gravely and intensely on communicating this stuff to him. It just sounded so much like psychobabble. Female psychobabble. And though he was happy listening to Rach's psychobabble anytime, he had no clue what any of this had to do with The Monica Problem.

"Okay. Forget talking. Just watch.'' Rach swiftly climbed to her feet, walked to the door and then spun around. Her expression had completely changed. Her shoulders drooped an inch or so. She glanced around the room, but with her eyes slightly downcast. She adjusted her sweater hem so that one side sagged unevenly. She pushed up imaginary glasses on her nose and then shuffled imaginary papers in her hands as if they were more important to her than anything else in sight. "Hi, there," she said, looked straight at him, smiled, then quickly returned her concentration back to her imaginary papers.

Greg scratched his chin. "Okay, okay, I get what you're showing me—someone with no confidence."

"Good. Now let me do it one more time." Again she walked to the door and spun around. Again her expression was significantly different. This time her posture was straight, her shoulders proud, tall. She glanced actively around the room as she hiked in a circle. Her sweater hem cuddled on her hips just so. She walked with a swing in her fanny. A delectable swing. "Hi there," she said, looked straight at him, smiled and let her imaginary papers fall to her side as if he were more important than any old work could be.

"Now do you see what I'm trying to show you?" she asked him. "I'm the same person. Nothing different about me physically. But that first walk—that's how I was right after divorcing Mark. It wasn't a conscious thing. But I was still giving other people messages that I didn't want to get too close. Friendly, yes. Close, no. And that's what I keep thinking, Greg, that you used to send a lot of keep-off signs before the accident."

"And now you think I walk with a swish in my behind?" he asked incredulously.

"No, you nut! Of course not! I was showing you examples from a girl's point of view, for Pete's sake. But what I'm trying to suggest is that maybe your life changed because of that accident. *Not* because you lost some weight and your face looks different. But because *you* changed. Maybe you're happier to be alive. Or just em-

bracing life more. The why doesn't matter. The point is
that when an incredible hunk is friendly to a woman, she's
programmed to think he's expressing sexual interest or
availability. And you're just sending out all these wonderful vibrant, virile messages these days. I'm not trying
to tease you, I swear. But whether you're intending to or
not, you could be sending out messages that you're available. And maybe that's partly what Monica's been picking
up on. Think about it, okay?''

She glanced at her watch and shrieked—then promptly
went into motion. Skirts swirled around her thighs. She
boogied around, pulling on her jacket, pushing on her
heels, getting the picnic basket ready. She had to be back
at work. ''This was just the first lesson,'' she told him
with a grin. ''And I want a full report on anything Monica
says to you this afternoon.''

Before she charged out, she bussed him with a kiss. On
his cheek. Just a smack. Translated, Greg figured it meant
I love you, good friend. Not *I'm crazy about you, lover.*

And then she was gone. He heard sounds pick up in
the outer office as his staff filtered back from lunch. Wes
showed up in his doorway, holding the payroll records.
''Do you have a minute, Mr. Stoner? I just came up with
a little problem I need to discuss with you—''

''I'm free in fifteen minutes. Hit me then, okay?''

He rolled his shoulders when he was alone again, thinking he needed those fifteen minutes to get his mind on
work. Right now there was only one thing in his head.
Rach. How she'd talked about sex, how she'd made the
sexy foods, how she'd hurled herself in his arms with
those overheated kisses. In principle, he knew, she was
only playing out the game to make Monica believe he had
a woman in his life. It was all for his sake. Something a
friend would do for another.

Only, too much had happened in the last few weeks for Greg to believe that.

Rach loved him. Or believed she did. It had nothing to do with the smoky perfume or the sexy sweater. It was the vulnerable, yearning way she was looking at him. It was the way her kisses started out playful and turned into something naked and soft and dark—real, real fast.

Greg had already told himself the obvious—that she was over Sacred Mark, up to looking for a mate again, and she only glanced his way because she trusted him. That wasn't love. It was testing her newfound confidence on someone who wouldn't hurt her if he could conceivably help it.

And maybe—if he wasn't so selfish—he'd make love with her. She seemed to want to. And her getting her feet wet sexually with a guy who deeply loved her wasn't the worst idea in town. He could do his best to make her feel wonderful about her femininity and sexuality. Possibly making love with a friend was the best thing that could happen to her right now.

The glitch was him. His own selfishness. Because his new face wasn't going to make a lick of difference when the lights went off. He was enjoying her treating him like a prince—he couldn't deny it. But when push came down to naked shove, he was the same old frog. He knew that. He'd faced that.

For once in his life, though—for Rachel—he just wanted to be that prince she believed in. If he handled this wrong, he was afraid of not only disappointing her—but of losing her forever.

Seven

For two years Rachel hadn't taken any serious risks. Certainly not the kind of risks that mattered. But now she leaned forward in front of her closet mirror, stuffed her breasts into a black velvet bra, hooked the clasp and then straightened up to judge the results.

Holy cow. Those bra ads actually came through with delivering a miracle. She actually looked as if she'd doubled her boob size. Of course, it was the effect of the wires, not her, but temporarily Rachel wasn't fussy about the details.

Greg was supposed to pick her up in another twenty minutes and she needed every second of that time to get ready—as in capital *R* Ready. She spun around, looking for the black lace garter belt and black seamed stockings.

Her mind should have been on the symphony they were attending tonight, not seducing Stoner. Symphony tickets were one of the perks Monica gave the company executives—Greg glumly told her it was an attend-or-die type of perk; nobody wanted to go, which was how he'd begged her into attending with him. Sooner or later the symphony would end, though, and then she'd have Stoner to herself.

Lunch last week had been the catalyst for this seduction plan, and it was entirely his own fault he had to suffer through this. She'd *only* brought the aphrodisiac foods and thrown herself in his lap as part of their game—a way to make Monica believe he was in an intimate, committed relationship. Stoner was supposed to laugh at her hammed-up vamp role. But nothing about those kisses had been humorous. He'd returned each kiss, each touch, as if he were sinking, drowning in her, going deep underwater where heat and need were deep and rich and pulse pounding. And then…he'd frozen up faster than an iceberg in the Arctic.

For four nights running, Rachel had tossed and turned how and why he would kiss her that way—and then back off. Memories kept festering in her mind. Her memories, not his. But after Mark picked up with another woman, she recalled feeling like a nothing, a failure, a fool and a total Sexual Zero if she'd been so easy to forget and throw away.

That hadn't happened in Greg's life—but she kept recalling how often he put himself down. He referred to himself as a dolt or a nerd, and for so many years had chosen haircuts and clothes that made him less attractive than he could be. That was the kind of thing *she'd* done when her confidence was at its lowest. And maybe Stoner turned cold because he simply didn't love her—but just maybe he did. Or could. If he could just see himself as a lover instead of a nerd.

She'd stewed on the problem all week now. Long—

long—before he started looking like George Clooney, Stoner was a good man. Strong, dynamic, principled. A hero and a lover both. But if the dimwit couldn't see that, conceivably he needed a nudge from a friend. Someone who'd helpfully seduce him. Who'd altruistically make him feel like a sexy, desirable man, and make absolutely sure he knew he was a prince of a darling instead of a darn fool nerd.

Rachel fully realized that her qualifications for this task were nominal—but obviously only a woman could do the job, and being a friend who'd never hurt him was an equally critical factor.

Finally she located the garter belt and stockings hiding in the folds of her comforter. This was for him, she firmly told herself as she started unraveling the seamed black silk stocking. That was her story and she was sticking to it.

She'd lose all her courage if she admitted there could conceivably be any other reason why she was doing this.

The alien garter contraption took a couple minutes to figure out, but she mastered the sucker just as the bedside telephone rang. She grabbed the receiver with a glance at the clock—Greg was now due in less than ten minutes. She had no time to dawdle or talk.

The caller was her mother. Dragging the receiver, Rach sprinted across the room to the closet. She pulled out her dress and shoes at the same time she girl-talked with her mom and simultaneously fretted how inappropriate her bedroom was for seducing anyone. Her comforter was in sherbet shades of cherry, tangerine and lime, the curtains and rocking chair seat a pale lime and the carpet a slightly darker hue. Everything was wrong. The room looked more like an ice cream-parlor than a lover's lair. And all the furniture was secondhand. And the bedside lamp was too bright. And she didn't have any candles up here. And...

Her mom's familiar voice pounced back into her consciousness. "So what are you up to tonight, sweetie?"

Hurriedly Rachel pushed her feet into teetering-tall black pumps and galloped—precariously—over to her jewelry box. "Nothing much. It's so freezing outside, I was just planning to snuggle up in front of the tube with a nice, warm bowl of oatmeal and some cocoa," she said virtuously.

"Oh my God. You're sleeping with someone."

Startled, Rachel dropped the long jet earring she'd been trying to plug into her ear one-handed. "Excuse me?"

"Give it up, girl. The oatmeal was a dead giveaway. Who is he?"

"Mom. I've told you a thousand times that I sleep around all the *time*—"

"And cats sing. Well, he'd better be good to you. If he's anything like Mark, your father will kill him. And after he does, I'll kill him all over again. What's he look like?"

"All right. The real truth is, I'm not eating a bowl of oatmeal. I'm going to the symphony. With a man. But I didn't want to tell you that because it's a courtesy date—he got stuck with two tickets he really didn't want—and I was afraid you'd jump to conclusions if I admitted going anywhere with a guy."

Her mother immediately simmered down and swallowed that story as a far more palatable truth. And then Rachel invited the clan for Thanksgiving next week, because there was no way her mom would hang up until the holiday plans were settled, nor was she willing to cook a turkey if there was any way out of it. Finally Rachel was able to sever the call, and then really had to fly.

The doorbell rang just as she was yanking the dress from its hanger. She yelled out, "Coming, Stoner!"

At least the dress was worth every dime she couldn't afford to pay for it—and just the confidence booster she needed. Eyes closed, she pulled the silky black fabric over her head, fit in the long sleeves, and then felt the material shiver over her breasts, slink down her hips, then settle with a swish above her knees.

From downstairs she suddenly heard Greg's humorous baritone. "Hey, are you alive up there?"

"I'm coming, I'm coming, honest!" Whirlwind fast, she jabbed two jet combs in her hair, sprayed on scent, brushed on shadow and lipstick and bronzer and grabbed her black velvet evening bag. Praying not to kill herself in the spike pumps, she hurled down the stairs, a radiant smile plastered on her mouth...until she spotted him.

Oh man. This was all wrong. She'd been crazy to think Greg needed her, crazy to think he could possibly have insecurities about being a lover. He looked fabulous—the height of confidence and pulse-kicking sex appeal. The black suit matched his glossy dark hair perfectly and showed off his wide shoulders, the white linen shirt such an elegant contrast against his ruddy skin.

Mentally she sucked in a breath. She'd already been suffering a volcano of nerves that she'd never be woman enough to pull this off—not a real, live, get-naked-in-a-bedroom seduction—but suddenly those volcanic nerves eased. Forget the seduction. She probably would have failed that miserably, anyway, but she was going to spend the evening with Stoner—which meant they were going to have a guaranteed great time just like always—if she just let it happen.

Anxiety disappeared from her pulse. Maybe the wires in her bra had faked her bustline, but her feelings for him certainly weren't fake. She loved that man. Her lips pursed—not to deliver a kiss—but to let out a good, long, teasing wolf whistle. "*Wow.* You're making my heart go pitty-pat. Who'd guess you'd clean up into such a sexy hunk?"

"Impressed, huh? Hey, impressed me, too. I nearly scared myself when I looked in the mirror at home," Greg said wryly. "Of course you picked out this suit. Even a bum looks pretty good or okay in a tux. Now you, on the other hand... That's quite a dress."

"Isn't it?" She twirled around at the bottom of the stairs—showing off—then swiftly buried her head in the hall closet and emerged with her black velvet wrap. "I'm ashamed what it did to my credit card, but what the hey. I don't splurge that often. Although it was so expensive I couldn't afford to wear anything underneath it."

Greg choked. "What'd you just say?"

She grinned as she whipped the wrap around her shoulders and headed for the door. "Just practicing giving you a heart attack. Did you think there'd be no payback for dragging me to this blasted symphony?"

"I thought you said you liked classical music."

"Well, I didn't want to make you feel guilty for asking me. I love symphonies the same way I love tetanus shots and brussels sprouts—but really, I'm glad to go. We'll have a good time with each other no matter what. And I figured when you called that you must have needed the moral support...although I started worrying that something else could have happened between you and Monica."

Outside, snowflakes were drifting down from the night sky like wet diamonds. The night was a ghostly ebony, the grass already stiffened into sharp frozen spears that glistened in the shadows. Greg ushered her into his car, and got the engine and heater going full blast before speaking again. "She makes a big deal out of the managers and executives attending these cultural events. Technically they're supposed to be treats, but when you're handed a ticket, you'd damn well better go."

"Yeah, you explained that before. What you didn't tell me was how she responded to you after our lunch last week."

Greg sighed. "Well…it went fine for about three days. I thought the problem was gone for good. But then I went into a budget meeting with her and three production supervisors, and under the table I felt these stocking toes climbing up my leg."

Rachel's head jerked in his direction. "Yikes. I guess it's obvious our little act didn't convince her that you and I were a couple?" Snow splattered on the windshield and instantly melted, making the lights of Milwaukee shimmer and glow as the car aimed downtown.

"Actually, I think it did convince her. It just seemed to bring out a competitive streak. The next day I attended a lunch meeting with her and John Gray, one of the firm's bankers. Only, John never showed. I think Monica deliberately told me the wrong date, because she started talking about you. She asked me what you liked in bed. Tried to tell me what kind of inventive things she liked, playing like she was counseling me on how to sexually please you."

"Jeez, Louise. That's not funny."

"I didn't think so, either. An off-color joke or occasional flirtatious comment is one thing, but…" He shook his head. "I shifted my chair away to avoid her damn foot. And said flat out that I didn't appreciate the nature of the conversation."

"To which she said…?"

"That I was being old-fashioned. We were both adults. And if I was serious about you, she could give me lessons on what it took to please a woman and no one would be the wiser. Not that I needed lessons, but no man thinks like a woman and she could give me an inside view. I said thanks, but you and I were doing terrific on our own."

"And that was the end of it?"

"Until she said she'd be sitting next to me at the symphony tonight. And that Dennis Stoddard was 'doing a fabulous job, wasn't he.'"

"I don't understand. Who's Dennis?"

"He's a young man in my department. I believe she was suggesting—or threatening—that if I don't play ball, she already has someone in mind to replace me. The funny thing is that Dennis had already been on my mind for the same reason. He's a fine man, bright, hard worker. I've groomed and worked with him since he hired on, so I know what he's capable of. Right now, I think he's too young to take over a financial department on his own...but I was still thinking about him as my replacement in case I had to quit."

Troubled, Rachel started to say, "Greg..."

"I was tempted to tell her where she could shove the job. And I still am. I'm not willing to sit here and take this nonsense much longer. But the thing is, Monica never started this until a few weeks ago. All this time we worked okay together. So if there's something I can do to turn it back around, I really want to try."

"I understand."

Greg glanced at her. "Rach, I'd appreciate your help, but not like last time. I put you in an uncomfortable position the other day without thinking. Playing lovers seemed like fun, no harm, no risk—but it still couldn't have been comfortable for you. Besides which, I'm a grown man and can rescue myself. What I'd appreciate from you is advice. How another woman would see her, judge her. I don't know whether to quit or sue her, ignore or confront her.''

Within minutes they were walking into the symphony. Rachel always thought of Milwaukee as a rambunctiously happy football and beer town, but the place was packed, and with an elegantly dressed crowd. Greg's co-workers were already there, taking their seats—and so was his boss.

Monica was dressed in a long, sweeping cranberry dress with a black velvet jacket, her hair swept up and doing the perfect dangling tendril thing, her makeup distinctively from the Saks cosmetic counter instead of the local drugstore. Rachel made a point of sitting between the boss and Greg, but as she could have guessed, Monica behaved like a perfect lady. She chatted up each of her staff, made small talk when appropriate, and in this public setting, naturally treated Greg no differently than anyone else.

Any other time, Rachel would have worried about falling asleep once the music started—classical had just never been her cuppa. Tonight, though, it wouldn't have mattered if her favorite R&B was playing. A disturbing drumbeat thrummed through her pulse. The cause was she was sitting next to Stoner, twining fingers with him, rubbing shoulders, catching the glint in his eyes when he smiled at her now and then.

He could stir the drumbeat in a nun's pulse.

Rachel shifted impatiently. Then shifted again. Maybe her mind had been dominated by sex earlier, but now she had a job to do. She couldn't afford to be thinking about loving Greg. Or about making love with him. There was a time for hormones and a time for worry, and this fit into the Worry Time.

He thought his problem was Monica. Rachel perceived exactly how serious the sexual harassment sweat with his boss was for him—and for the threat to his job. But as she saw it, the real problem was Greg himself.

All week she'd been concluding the same thing, just from a different angle. Greg didn't see himself as a lover. It completely bewildered him that any woman did.

He was absolutely determined that the few changes to his face done by the plastic surgeon were the only reason women were noticing him—which was downright crazy. He'd always been a darling man whom women had liked and respected and trusted. Before the surgery, though, he'd made appearance choices that made it easy for him to hide from attention. The extra weight and sloppy way of wearing clothes effectively advertised that he was unattractive and unlovable.

God knew, Rachel remembered a time in her life when she'd felt exactly the same way about herself—and used similar methods to send keep-out signals. But that wasn't the point. Stoner was the point. How to understand him. How to help him. And what someone who loved him would do for Greg in these circumstances.

What he'd asked her to do, of course, was to form some feminine impressions about Monica—but that was easy. A trip to the ladies' room invariably involved some girl talk; she had another chance during the intermission, and once the symphony ended, the women had a general talk-fest in the lobby while the men braved the snowy night to fetch the cars.

When Greg finally pulled up with his black Volvo, the midnight sky was dumping silver sleet in buckets. She raced to jump in and huddle under the heater's blast.

"Had enough classical music to last you awhile?" he asked wryly.

"Actually, no. It hurts to eat crow, but I have to admit I really loved it. Come on, didn't you? In fact, I loved it so much that if it came down to a choice between season tickets for the symphony versus football—"

He shot her a horrified look. "Hell. Don't go too high-brow on me."

She chuckled. "As if I'd be disloyal to our Packers. I'd sit in a blizzard for a Green Bay game." But it was so easy to keep up a teasing banter with him. She sobered quickly. "I had quite a few chances to talk with Monica."

"I know you did. And I appreciate it, Rach. So…what'd you think? Come up with any new ideas for me?"

"Well, yes and no. A bunch of ideas are spinning in my mind…but I need a couple minutes to sort them out before trying to talk, okay?"

"Sure." He didn't press, just shot a quick glance at her face, then concentrated on driving. He needed to. Fall had turned into winter overnight—not untypical of Milwaukee—but the night had turned seriously mean. The roads were slick, the sky clogged with snow-swollen clouds and the sleet kept coming down in sharp, driving sheets.

The minute he pulled into her driveway, she reached for the car door handle. "Come on in. I'll make some tea or chocolate or a drink. Something to warm us up."

Although the hour was late, he didn't object to coming in. She unlocked the back door and suggested he plunk comfortably on the couch in the living room while she foraged for drinks. She dropped her velvet wrap and bag, flipped on the squint-bright kitchen light, then poured something gold for Stoner and a small burgundy for herself. Pensively she stalled in the kitchen for just a few more seconds. She knew what she wanted to communicate to Greg. Just not if she could do it well.

She kicked off her heels and padded in, carrying both glasses. Predictably Greg hadn't settled down and relaxed; she found him hunkered down at her hearth, trying to coax some kindling to life. He loved a fire, had one going at her place as often as he did at his own. This particular baby-size blaze, though, would seem a clear indication he didn't plan to stay long. When he spotted her in the doorway, he lurched to his feet and immediately reached for a lamp switch. Rachel figured that was another sign he really wasn't looking for an intimate atmosphere, but she asked him not to turn on the lamp.

"This is probably going to sound goofy," she admitted, "but what I want to talk to you about is awkward for me. I'd rather keep the lights off and just talk by firelight, if you don't mind."

"Of course I don't mind. But you don't need to feel awkward with me, Rach. You know better. We've talked about everything under the sun together."

Rachel dropped down next to him on the hearth, tucking her legs beneath her, thinking that was how it used to be between them—absolutely no subject taboo, no nerves infecting their friendship. But as she'd discovered for weeks now, love screwed up everything. Now those gorgeous blue eyes short-circuited her brain cells, and his physical closeness gave her flu symptoms, and she just couldn't seem to feel sure of anything anymore. Except that loving Stoner meant wanting to do the right thing for him—even if that meant risk for her.

"You asked me for advice," she said quietly.

"Yes—"

"Well, I think what Monica is doing to you is straight sexual harassment. It's wrong. I think you could win if you sued her. I also think, if you just choose to quit, you could find another job you loved in about five seconds flat. You know you're terrific at your work, Stoner. And you also know that you have a super reputation in your field. But you want a different solution than those choices, don't you? Because you don't want to either quit or sue.''

''Right, on both counts.'' Greg cocked up a knee, looking at her instead of the fire.

She looked at the fire instead of him. ''Greg...I don't doubt she'd like to mess around with you. But in any of those encounters, did you see anything to make you think you've suddenly turned into the love of her life, the sun and the moon, that kind of serious emotional feeling?''

''No,'' he said thoughtfully, and then stronger, ''no, nothing like that. These have been straight sexual passes. Nothing more.''

Rachel nodded. ''That was my impression, too. She wants you. But that's not the same thing as thinking she'll happily tear up her whole life to get you. More like she's a competitive woman with a lot of pride. So she has an allergy to the word *no*. And she hates backing down once she's made a move, even if she realizes that move was a mistake. Even considering that stuff, though—in my opinion—this could blow over. If one of two things happen.''

''And those two things are?'' he probed.

''I suspect that Monica, being Monica, needs to be able to save face. Having a guy in her life would do that—but that isn't something you could fix. What might really help bring her around, though, is an attitude change from you.''

He leaned forward with a startled expression. ''From me? What kind of attitude change? Are you saying I'm at fault—?''

''Good grief, no. She's the only one at fault here. Not you. But...''

"But what?"

Rachel met his eyes, saw his rumpled hair catch the gleam of firelight, caught the sharp profile of his cheek and jaw, and wanted to touch him—not talk. For sure she didn't want to bring up issues that could discourage him from ever thinking of her in a romantic light. She tugged on an earring from nerves. "Stoner," she said slowly, "I watched her watching you tonight. I also watched you being scrupulously polite, sending her keep-off messages right and left. She knows when she's making you uneasy. And I think that's the main problem. Some people are just predators, vulturelike. She senses a sore and goes right for that vulnerable spot."

He shook his head. "I don't get what you mean. I don't have any 'sore.'"

"Well, let me explain what kind of sore I'm talking about." She hesitated. "When Mark first left me, I quit wearing makeup for a while. Only wore oversize clothes. Avoided any guy who dared smile at me."

Greg clearly didn't see how his problem with Monica related to the change of subject, but his tone gentled and quieted. "I remember what a tough time you were going through when you first moved here," he affirmed. "And I think it's real understandable that you didn't feel like trusting men for a while."

"No. That wasn't the problem." She sighed. This was the hard part. Exposing those humiliating feelings again. Especially to Greg. "For months I dressed to be invisible—not because I was afraid some guy would ask me out. But because I didn't want anyone to look too close and realize I was poison."

"Poison?"

"For a long time, that's what I thought. In theory, I knew Mark was the jerk, not me. He had the character of a turnip. I was better off without him. But on the inside, when he took off with another woman, I just felt so…forgettable. I'd loved him. Given him everything I was, everything I had. And if he could walk away from me that easily, I figured I had to be a failure deep on the inside. Sexually, emotionally and every other way.''

''Hey, cut it out. I hate your remembering how bad that creep made you feel back then—''

''Yeah, well, so do I. But the point is, I remember the symptoms. I felt like I was poison. Like something had to be wrong with me. In bed and out of it. And I was scared of letting any man get close enough to figure it out. That I was a zero underneath.''

''Rachel—''

Even in the shadows, she could see his shoulders stiffening and his jaw tightening. Stoner hated it when she talked herself down, so before he could say anything, she interjected swiftly, carefully, ''Greg, I'm not knocking myself for the thrill of it, but to make a point. I'm saying, I *know* those feelings. I recognize those symptoms. And I'm not the only one who has them.''

''Huh? I don't understand what you mean—''

''My problem was Mark, and a divorce that knocked all the confidence out of me. I don't know what happened to you—and you don't have to tell me,'' she said softly. ''But something did.''

He shook his head as if trying to clear liquid from his ears. ''Where on earth would you get that impression?''

''Because. You're a fantastic man. Warm, intelligent, funny. Caring. Responsible. And yeah, you're good-looking, too. But there's a reason Monica is choosing now to pick on you—and it has nothing to do with the way the plastic surgeon rearranged a couple of little bones.''

"I have a feeling you're going to tell me this startling reason," he said dryly.

She nodded. "Yes. The doctor took off your mask, Stoner. You always wore invisible clothes, walked in a nondescript way. When I really think about it, you worked like a dog to make people—especially women—think you were dull. Boring."

A confused frown pleated his brow for several moments, and then he turned to stoke the fire with a poker. "Rach. That was no *mask*. It was me. The truth. I was never a swashbuckling Errol Flynn kind of guy. I *am* dull and ordinary."

"And there's the sore," Rachel murmured.

"Huh?"

"I don't know who hurt you. And I don't give a damn. But we're going to get this straight right now," she said fiercely. "You're *not* dull, you nimwit. You're an extraordinary man. A take-charge hero type all day. You're superkind and patient with all kinds of people—like Josie and old Mr. Rembrowsky—and people like me. We started out strangers, yet you still went out of your way to help me. Everybody knows they can come to you. People at your work, people in the neighborhood. You've got character and heart and guts. And even more important— to a woman—is that you're a a grown-up, for Pete's sake."

"Um, in case you haven't noticed, most people over twenty-one are."

"Nope, they're not. Not men. " She was warming up now, the blood pumping, her nurturing instincts on full charge. She was getting through to him. His throat wouldn't be that dull brick red if she weren't. "There are tons of guys who don't want to grow up. My ex was one of them. He really thought his selfishness and irresponsibility were boyish and charming. As if a real man would never choose to commit to anything. As if honor and integrity and all that stuff is hopelessly dull—''

"Okay, okay. I hear you. But you happened to be married to an immature dweeb, Rach. And no, I don't think integrity is dull. But that doesn't change reality, that some men are simply on the dull, staid side—''

"My God, it's like trying to get through to a rock." She scalped a hand through her hair in frustration. "You've got an MBA from Wharton, so you'd think there'd be a brain in that noggin. But you haven't understood one word I've said, have you?"

"Yes, I have. Of course I have. But I don't understand what any of this has to do with Monica—''

"It has everything to do with her. You can't change her attitude unless you understand what's inspiring her to act this way. And that's the nutshell. I've been trying to tell you *why* she's hitting on you, Stoner."

"Because I got a new face."

"No."

"Because I'm better looking than I used to be."

"No," she repeated impatiently.

"Then why?"

"Because you're *lovable,* you nimwit! And it's not like women didn't realize that before, but the surgeon stripped off your mask. And then you lost the extra weight, and started walking and dressing different, and the whole invisible thing you used to hide behind is gone. Nothing is really new, except that it's easier to see you're a lovable, adorable, heroic kind of guy. You were hiding it so deeply—''

"Uh, Rach? I think that half a glass of wine must have gone straight to your head."

The wine hadn't. But he had. Somehow, some way, she

was going to force that man to see himself as lovable or die trying. "That's *it!* I give up! I was afraid that talking was just a waste of time. Obviously there's only one thing that's going to get through to you, Stoner, and I swear, you aren't giving me any choice but to show you—"

Eight

When Rach suddenly climbed to her feet, Greg felt a huge sigh of relief. He didn't know whether she was headed for the kitchen or bathroom, nor did he care.

He squeezed his eyes closed, grateful that he was about to be blessed with a few seconds alone. This whole conversation had gotten away from him. Hell, the whole evening had gone completely wrong. He just needed a minute to figure out why—and what to do about it.

When he'd asked Rachel to attend the symphony tonight, it had seemed like such a brilliant plan. Something drastic had to happen since their last lunch. Hormones couldn't keep exploding between them. That way lay Armageddon.

Using the symphony and his problems with Monica had seemed the ideal answer. Truthfully his boss was starting to drive him bonkers—if she couldn't keep her red talons off his butt, and soon, Greg was going to have to tactfully suggest a sunless place where she could stuff the job. But that was his problem, not Rachel's. He'd only given Rachel the impression he needed her help for a specific purpose—to put their relationship back on a friendship footing.

Would she feel attracted to a weak, inadequate toad? No. Would an alpha guy get himself embroiled in a humiliating problem such as a woman he couldn't handle? No. Did hunks need rescuing? No. Ergo, this evening's excursion should have easily, gently and painlessly underlined for Rach that he was a dolt—and not remotely the kind of mate she was looking for.

And maybe it had. Only, he couldn't keep his mind on the job. She looked so breathtaking in that sin-black dress. She was a walking advertising for temptation, between that hip-swishing walk, and the scent hovering kiss—close to her throat, and the dark fire in her eyes when she looked at him—looking as if she wanted him, as if she'd cared. And then they'd come home, and all she'd been indirectly talking about was sex, the kind of things that turned her on in a man—*not* the best subject for him to keep a level head. Worse yet, she'd brought up Sacred Mark, which always sharpened the knives on his nerves, because he hated how that son of a sea dog had crushed her feminine confidence....

Suddenly color flashed behind his closed eyelids, startling him. The instant his eyes shot open, his forehead creased in a confused frown. Bare seconds before, he'd assumed Rachel had left the room.

It seemed...she hadn't.

It seemed...she was moving. At rocket-launch speed. Toward him.

The last he remembered, she'd been insulting him and calling him an idiot and muttering about having to *show* him what she meant about something or other. Certainly there was nothing to clue him in to what she was doing now. It wasn't an unusual conversation. She was invariably correcting him about something. She was female, after all.

Still, there did seem to be something different in this circumstance.

Drastically different.

A hundred and ten pounds suddenly landed with breathtaking enthusiasm—on him. Physical contact was precisely what he'd been trying to avoid…and this was like an addict immersed in his favorite Uncontrolled Substance. A silky mouth smashed against his. Soft curves and soft flesh propelled him back against the rough carpet nap, inches from their sleepy little fire. Slim legs hooked around him, making folds of skirts whisper and rustle around his thighs, a knee threatening his future children, and the view of one shadowed breast threatening his sanity.

It was the she-made-me-do-it fantasy come to life. Only, it was better than a fantasy because it was Rachel, not some damn fool imaginary goddess, but his love goddess for real. When her tousled head blocked the firelight, there was nothing but velvet darkness and those lush, drugging, dizzying kisses of hers.

And his conscience.

"Rach? I—"

"Don't talk, Stoner," she muttered fiercely. "We tried talking. You didn't get it." She attacked again with more pouncing, bouncing kisses…kisses concentrated with far more determination than ardor. Yet he tasted the ardor. He tasted the undiluted emotion pouring from her. And he could feel himself already swimming in her taste, her scent, her textures.

"Didn't get...what?''

"You're *not* a nerd.''

This announcement struck him as fascinating, but seemed to have no relationship to why she'd suddenly launched herself at him like a spontaneous catapult. Before he got sucked under a third time, he tried a desperate "I don't think this is a good idea.''

"I do.''

"Rach, you can't be sure. I can feel your hands trembling—''

"Well, of course, they are. I haven't made love with anyone since I was married. And Mark made me feel like I was a zero. Maybe I am a zero. If so, you're really going to suffer through a long night.''

"You're *not* a zero.'' He swallowed hard when she took a small bite out of his right ear. "And someone who's close to you—who cares—is a natural person to turn to when you're testing out your sexual confidence again.''

"I love it when you lecture me in that careful, pedantic tone of voice. It makes me so hot.''

Better if he pretended not to hear that. "I was trying to make you think.''

"I'm sick of thinking. I want to make love. With you, only with you. Don't you want me?''

Only nonstop. Only like a clawing from the inside out. Only like a knife-edged need that had been building from the day he met Rach.

Only, she wasn't supposed to know that.

"I want you,'' he admitted with careful truth, "but—''

"Well, good. You know where my bedroom is.'' She twisted off his lap and stood up, pulling at his hands. Although he never meant to stand up, suddenly he was. And although she didn't have the physical strength of a pipsqueak, somehow she was pulling him along with no trouble at all. That didn't mean he'd completely lost his mind, though.

"Of course I know where your bedroom is. I've painted walls and done storm windows with you more than once. But I think we should talk about this—"

"I'm talked-out." At the base of the stairs, she seemed to be walked-out, too, and concentrated all her attention on attacking him again. Soft, slow, exploring fingers flipped open his shirt buttons, one, then two, then Yikes. She flipped open the waist button of his pants.

"Now, Rach. Just take it easy—" He wasn't exactly following her up the stairs. But he had to be close enough to reason with her.

"I've got condoms somewhere in my room. I bought them the day I got divorced. A box. A big box. I was going to go out and sleep instantly with five hundred men right then, one after the other, get over the creep come hell or high water. At the time it seemed like such a great idea, but I don't know, I just never got around to it. And now it's been so long that I'm not dead sure where the box even is—"

"I thought you didn't want to talk."

"This isn't talking. It's nervous chattering. I'm scared witless, Stoner. Can't you do something about that?"

"There isn't any way you could be scared of me," he assured her.

"Yeah, there is."

"What. What do you think you're scared of?"

"That you'll think my hips are too fat."

"Your hips are perfect." He used that lecturing, pedantic tone again—just so she'd pay attention.

"You'll think I'm too small on the upstairs deck."

"Small-breasted women are the sexiest. Everybody knows that." Again he used the voice of authority.

"Maybe I won't kiss right."

"We've already kissed. If you kissed any better, I'd get electrocuted from the voltage."

The softest of smiles, luring him, tempting him closer. "Oh, Stoner. You are so good to me. But I'm serious about being worried. I just can't seem to be the kind of person who gets naked easily. I love you," she mentioned. "You'd think that would help, but instead it makes it worse. If we were strangers, it wouldn't matter if this goes terribly. But everything matters so much more when you love someone. In fact, the more I worry, the more I—"

Damned if he knew how they made it to the pitch-dark hall outside her bedroom. He was positive he'd never intended to go upstairs. Positive he had no intention of making love with her. Positive he never planned to kiss her.

Yet his mouth lanced on hers with deliberate and searing pressure. He had to. He hadn't heard her talk herself down that way since Sacred Mark first left. He never wanted her worried about her sexual or feminine confidence ever again.

Possibly that didn't precisely explain why he backed her against a bedroom wall and started kissing her senseless, but the logical part of his mind malfunctioned, then stalled out completely. The instant he initiated those first kisses, her arms skimmed up and around his neck and her spine bowed to invite further body contact. He could feel the pounding of her heartbeat, the crushing swell of her breasts against his chest, the quiver of muscle in her legs as she surged up on tiptoe to meet his kisses.

He lifted her, making a sling of his arms under her fanny, feeling his fresh-healed ribs groan even though she was a lightweight—but they had to move. Standing-up kisses just weren't working. Not anymore. Basically he knew her bedroom layout, remembered the ice cream colors from when he'd helped her paint the walls and lay the carpet. But it was too dark for him to make out shapes. Outside, the snowstorm had intensified. Inside, floorboards creaked and the wind moaned in trapped crevices and nothing but wild, bully-black shadows reflected from her one tall bedroom window. He couldn't turn on a light. His mouth was latched on hers tighter than a key glued in its lock.

Five minutes ago, not touching her may have been an option.

That option had disappeared.

His knee connected with the bed edge. He wanted to drop her on the mattress and follow her down, yet latently he remembered her dress. A good dress. Too good to risk her getting distracted, worrying about it. So he loosened his hold, set her on her feet, spun her around. In the dark, his fingers felt like fumbling giants, trying to cope with the itty-bitty unseen zipper tip. Yet he found it. And everything in the room seemed gloomy black but her silver-white skin as he peeled the zipper down, trailing kisses on every inch of warm, pearly flesh he uncovered.

Eventually, with a little assistance, the dress swooshed to the ground. "Greg?"

She hadn't turned around yet, but he heard her breathing sound suddenly uneasy, nervous. Hell, she should be nervous. The spindly scrap of black velvet was barely a bra, and he saw the black lace garter belt with the silk stockings. He just didn't see anything underneath it.

She turned around, her face tilted to his. "I wore the lingerie for you," she confessed.

"You wanted me to have a heart attack?"

"Yeah. I was hoping you'd have a little one."

"I'd have had a huge one if I'd realized you weren't wearing underpants all evening. Rach?"

"What?"

"You're in trouble."

He heard her wicked, responsive chuckle, before he swooped down on her mouth again. His mind started spinning like a whirling dervish, sensations and feelings tumbling into each other, invoked—provoked—by the emotions coming off from her. In that cool, dark, drafty room, she was the only warmth. He drank in her kisses, sinking into her as if he were sinking into a warm, silky lake, feeling liquid, feeling weightless, feeling the scent of her roar in his ears. He tasted her breathy sighs, inhaled her impatience. Her hands were pushing at his shirt, trying to pull it off, trapping the material around his wrists, while her lips flashed fire on his skin with kisses on his throat and chest.

He yanked the shirt free, hurled it, then lowered her to the bed. A soft cushioned quilt draped the surface, cool to the touch, an exquisite contrast to her hot skin. Her breasts swelled, pushing against the confines of the black velvet bra, offering him a delectable edge to tease with his tongue. She shifted restlessly, trying to twist a leg around him, her stocking leg slinking, sliding evocatively against his pants fabric...a sensation that about blew the lid off his sanity. Nothing. There was nothing between them but his pants, and God knew he could get rid of those faster than the speed of light—assuming he was willing to let go of her for just a couple of seconds.

Which, unfortunately, he wasn't.

The craziest thing started happening, and kept happening. He was no Hotsy-totsy lover, never had been. He'd been in enough relationships to know he'd never earned any honors grades beneath the sheets. Only, something was eerie. He wasn't so klutzy. He wasn't so tense. Possibly his having a new face and leaner body had actually changed who he was, but he felt like a different man. Her man. The thing was, Rach was responding to him as if he were the most luscious sexy hunk in the universe. She acted as if she'd never wanted a guy, ever, like she wanted him, right-now-and-quit-messing-around.

The strangest thing of all was feeling his old, chronic fears of disappointing her seep away. All he really felt was increasingly sucked under. Good or bad didn't matter. Past or future didn't matter. His performance didn't matter. Nothing mattered except for her, and savoring every instant of these moments he had with her.

"Rach. You said you had protection," he murmured. Her eyes fluttered open, staring at him blankly in the darkness as if he'd mentioned something as irrelevant as the mathematical equation for the black hole. "If you don't remember where it is, it's all right. Trust me. We'll find another way."

"I don't want another way, Stoner. I want it the same old way lovers have liked it from the beginning of time. You, inside me, part of me. The drawer. Your side of the bed. The box has to be in there. There isn't any other place I'd have put it."

He reached out. The drawer creaked open. His fingers fumbled around shapes and textures, finally connecting with the box of protection. Technically it would have been so much easier to find it if he'd just switched on a light, but his gaze was mesmerized by the look of her face. His pupils had long dilated to compensate for the dark room by then, and snow was increasingly piling in the windowsill, reflecting light, reflecting sterling silver and soft gold shadows. All on her. Her eyes were liquid with emotion, her lips moist, her cheeks flushed like fever with desire.

He hustled off the rest of his clothes. Maybe leaving a sock. He wasn't sure. He couldn't stop looking at her, and when he was free enough to maneuver and had the annoying protection taken care of, he pinned her hands over her head. He considered divesting her of the garter belt and fancy bra but thought better of it. Maybe she'd bought the wicked lingerie to tease him, but he was challenged to discover if it could work the other way to bring out the wicked in her.

He started kissing the top of her head, then meandered down to her nose, her mouth, her throat, down to the delicious dip between her breasts and then further to rim a circle of kisses around her navel. She wasn't sure about her hands being held by then. He was. He aimed farther down, thinking possibly she was too shy for the most intimate kind of kisses, especially with a lover she didn't know...but he might only have this one time. One chance to prove that she could absolutely trust him, one chance to show her how love opened up her choices—and his.

One of his strengths in life had always been the ability to immerse himself in a task and give it his complete devotion.

For someone who'd been married, she seemed unfamiliar with her own sensuality, suddenly unsure, anxious—shy...but not for long. Her muscles clenched around him, reaching for the stroke of his hand, his tongue, small sounds aching from her throat that spoke of need and frustration and willful pleasure.

Man, this was fun.

More fun than he'd ever dreamed. Until she suddenly vaulted on top of him and ironed her mouth on his, with her finger clenched in his hair—as if she were trying to be positive she'd caught his attention ''You think you're the only one who gets to play down and dirty, Stoner,'' she whispered in a throaty hiss.

Truth to tell, he wasn't thinking at all. A sharp-edged hunger was scraping at his nerves. His jaw locked tight in desperation. She dazzled him, she always had, but his desire for her was two long, long years old…his yearning for her maybe older than he was. He really wanted to know how many times he could shatter a climax out of her, and was more than willing to try all night…but every muscle in his body felt like unconnected live wires, sizzling and snapping without being able to plug into an electric current. And that electric current seemed to have her name on it.

She seemed to like it that way. She bent her head, smiling a kiss on his lips, first sharing softness…then fire. When he swept her beneath him, she wrapped her legs around his waist, tensed in anticipation of his probing entry. She was hot, wet for him, her supple flesh yielding as if they were made for each other. Desire turned into a silent scream, clawing at his heart. The feel of her was beyond exquisite, beyond intimate. He no longer cared what happened after this. Loving her was worth any risk he'd ever taken, ever could take.

He wasn't a frog when he was with her. He wasn't himself. He was no one and nothing but her lover, and nothing in heaven and hell mattered more than pleasing her, loving her, cherishing her. They climbed, seeking and reaching for the same, not an end to this frustrated desire, but a beginning of something else between them…and there it was, a tip over the edge into a lush, soft oblivion, her crying his name at the same time he groaned, ''I love you, Rach. Love you, love you…''

But later he wondered if she'd heard him—because

nothing was the same between them again. Which was both wonderful.

And petrifying.

Certain Thanksgiving traditions seemed inescapable anywhere. Rachel, wearing giant blue oven mitts, crouched down in front of the oven door, trying to read the thermometer stuck in the plump, browning bird. From the living room, she suddenly heard Greg bellow a four letter word—followed by her father yelling a stream of profanities.

Her mother promptly showed up in the doorway. "Men are disgusting," Carolina announced.

As if this were news. "I take it the Lions are trying to ruin the boys' Thanksgiving by having the nerve to score against our Green Bay?" Rachel asked.

Her mom nodded. "We were only a field goal behind, but then Detroit scored another touchdown. The boys are taking this as if it were a personal affront. And I had instructions to ask if you could hold the turkey until half-time...."

"In their dreams." Rachel delicately raised her voice. "Turkey waits for no man. And for darn sure, I'm not risking a dried up bird just to cater to a silly old football game—"

"*Please,* Rach, my darling, the love of my life!" came a begging, seductive voice from the living room. A side-kick echoed, "Just for a few minutes, my most beautiful and favorite daughter—"

"You guys either come in when I call you, or you die." Rach pushed the swinging kitchen door closed, effectively muffling the sound of both bribes and swearing. "Both of them are pitiful. But just for the record, I planned the dinner for halftime."

Her mother laughed. "I always did, too. But you really can't count on a turkey to behave any more than you can a man. I always liked to let the boys worry, besides." Carrying a glass of cider, Carolina ambled around. "You've gone to so much trouble. And the table looks fabulous, hon."

Her kitchen table, truth to tell, was a door—but spiffed up with a fancy linen tablecloth and heirloom china, the effect was downright elegant. The sterling and china goodies had all come from her mom, who hustled—years ago—to give away anything that could force her to cook for more than two.

Rach pulled the heavy turkey out of the oven, sprinkled paprika on the top and then basted one last time, figuring the big baby would be done in about twenty more minutes. There were only five hundred things to do in the kitchen until then, but she took the time to study her mom. Carolina was adorable. A Meg Ryan's mom lookalike. No bigger than a button, with short, swingy blond hair and big beautiful eyes, today wearing brown pants that showed off her cute little butt, and an oversize orange sweater with a turkey on it.

One of these days she was going to be a hell-on-wheels grandma, Rachel mused affectionately. Carolina was probably the best mom who ever walked the earth, and easily had enough love to grandma a good dozen hellions. Unfortunately that was exactly what she wanted. Yesterday.

"Greg talks to your dad as if they were raised in the same disgusting back alley," Carolina remarked humorously.

"I noticed the same thing. Of course, you put men in front of a sports event, and their language and manners always instantly deteriorate. I think it's some kind of primitive regression.'' Rachel kept her voice light. Both her parents knew Greg well from previous visits, but they specifically did not know that their daughter had slept next door for the last five nights straight. If her mother knew the relationship had changed, ten thousand questions would immediately have followed. Maybe twenty thousand.

Anxiety and doubts suddenly squirmed in her stomach. Rach wouldn't have minded the questions…if only she had the answers. The last week had been the best of her life, including every one of those unforgettable nights. She regretted nothing. But Greg had said nothing about the future…possibly because he didn't want one. Not with her. The incredible change in their relationship was still new. She told herself it was reasonable, not cowardly, to just wait and be quiet and give Stoner time. Because her world had been rocked right side up didn't mean that his had been.

''Are you getting hungry, Mom?'' The innocuous question was much safer waters than anything to do with her next-door neighbor, Rachel mused.

''Starved.'' Carolina crunched down on a celery stick stuffed with cream cheese and chives, effectively ruining a beautifully arranged dish of hors d'oeuvres. ''Is that a new sweater? That shade of green's a terrific color for you.''

''Not brand-new. Thanksgiving Day cooking is so messy that I was afraid I'd ruin anything new.'' Damn, the bird's thermometer just popped. Swiftly she lugged the turkey to the stovetop, then checked on the marsh-mallow-glazed sweet potatoes. They could burn faster than a blink if not ruthlessly watched.

''New haircut?''

''Uh-huh.''

"Well, it looks wonderful, too. " Carolina's gorgeous blue eyes shrewdly trailed her daughter. "I keep trying to figure out what's different about you. Something is. Not the clothes, not the haircut. You look…glowing."

"Mom, I just took a twenty-pound turkey out of the oven! Naturally I'm glowing. It's warm in here!" Trying to divert her mother's attention, Rachel started giving her jobs. First she handed Carolina the cranberry-orange relish, then asked her to slice the corn bread. It didn't work.

"I worry about you," she announced.

"Well, that's pretty silly. I'm happy, healthy as a horse, doing great with my job…and you just finished telling me that I'm looking good—"

"And you are. Looking wonderful. But even when you were a little girl, you'd never tell us about a problem unless we pried it out of you. You think I don't know how bad Mark hurt you, but I saw. So did your father. Neither of us thought he was half good enough for you, even long before the divorce. "

Rachel knew. It was the main reason she'd moved to Milwaukee after Mark took off. Her parents loved her— so much that they'd have spoon-fed her money and love and sympathy forever if she'd let them. Rachel had needed to be on her own to stand on her own. And though it hadn't been obvious to her at the time, she needed to kick herself in the keester far more than she needed spoon-fed sympathy.

Carolina astutely relocated on the other side of the counter by the pecan and pumpkin pies—away from the work. She sampled a pecan, watching her daughter mash potatoes. From scratch yet. "You know, I'd believe you'd finally recovered from El Creepo…if I just knew there was a man in your life."

"I don't need a man to make me happy."

"No, of course, you don't. No one else can make you happy. It has to come from the inside." Carolina rolled her eyes. "God, I sound like one of those pop psychology books. But I'm still telling you straight. Life's no fun without sex. Without babies. Without a man swearing at football games in the other room—it's hard to explain. They're a terrible pain, but life's still better with them."

"I keep telling you I'm having wild, unprotected, impulsive sex all the time."

"Uh-huh. And I've tried to believe you. But you didn't have that different look in your eyes...until today." Carolina reached to steal another tidbit from the pecan pie, until Rachel batted her hand. "So...is the new guy good in bed?"

Rachel sighed. Only her mom would ask such questions—and expect to live. And her mom was mostly teasing. She didn't expect answers, but she did want reassurances that her life was on track, so Rachel tried to give those to her. "I felt wounded after Mark left me. I admit it. And I'm ashamed how long it took me to get over him, particularly when he was the one who cheated, not me. But it's over now completely, Mom. Honest."

"If it was over completely, I'd think there would be another man in your life right now."

"And maybe there could be. But at my age—and after a blooper the size of a divorce—I think the idea is to act like a grown-up and be more cautious and selective."

"Selective is fine," Carolina agreed, "but you know the old saying. Sometimes you have to kiss a few frogs to find the prince."

"Yeah, well, I thought Mark *was* a prince once upon a time. He didn't look like a spoiled, overindulged selfish jerk. He looked like a good guy. Talk about a frog who was parading as a prince...." That won a wry grin from her mother, and then Rachel quickly brought out her great-grandmother's infamous carving knife. ''Ask the guys to come in, will you? I'm counting on one of them being willing to carve.''

For the next ten minutes she raced around faster than a cat with hot feet, but it wasn't the holiday dinner that dominated her thoughts. The minute Greg ambled in, her heart swelled like a joyously inflated balloon. But fears and doubts squirmed around all that hope in her heart.

Vaguely she remembered back in the days when she thought she was a sexually desirable cookie. When sex was fun. When it never even occurred to worry about whether she was good at it. Experimenting was fun in itself; so were savoring those secret intimate moments and the laughter in the dark and everything else.

But she'd closed up tighter than a drum for years. And she'd blamed Mark for crippling her confidence, but that wasn't precisely true. She'd no longer trusted her emotional judgment. She doubted her ability to lure. To please. To keep. And was terribly afraid of humiliating herself by clinging to another man who didn't love her.

Greg cared about her. She was positive of that. She also felt secure that he loved her—at least a kind of love— and that he would never intentionally hurt her.

But the thing was, she hadn't been worried about her confidence or her sex appeal five nights ago. Not really. Somehow she'd talked herself into believing that making love was an important way she could help the man she loved...because Stoner had this dimwit idea that he was a nerd, and she wanted him to see himself as a desirable lover. Because he had some unspoken insecurities about his looks—especially since the plastic surgery—and she felt a loving friend could help him work through that stuff.

Only, now Rachel realized what a ball of horseradish she'd been selling herself.

Of course she'd wanted to help Greg. But she'd also hoped that making love would wake him up, put a boing in his noggin, make his heart lightbulb switch on. She'd hoped to hear him say "I love you"—not in the dark— but in the light. She'd hoped he'd start talking about hope. She'd hoped that he'd finally see that the two of them were and always had been immeasurably special together.

As a lover, Stoner was a true holy-kamoly. She couldn't imagine a man more imaginative or giving—or red-hot— than Greg when he took her in his arms. But Rachel couldn't forget how long she'd humiliated herself with her ex-husband, blindly believing Mark loved her, blindly believing Mark had feelings for her that he never had.

The sudden sound of boisterous conversation made her spin around as Greg finished carving the turkey and everyone settled down, oohing and aahing at the table and the bird. Even with her mom and dad right there, though, Rachel's eyes found Greg's the way lovers hopelessly radar-ed on each other. Delight was in his gaze. Intimate secrets. Wicked promises for the next time they were completely alone. And the palest rose brushed up her cheeks just from looking at him.

Yet all he said was, "You're all done working, princess. Your dad and I agreed we've been lolling like slugs, but we'll do the dishes and all the cleanup after. How's that?"

She shrieked from shock, like she was expected to. And through the exuberant holiday dinner, she treated Greg the way she'd always treated him—as a friendly neighbor, for her parents' sake. But her heart seemed to be coiling tighter and tighter by the hour.

If he didn't love her, she'd started something that could lead to disaster. She'd never survive just having an affair with him. And if that was all Greg wanted from her, she was in deep emotional trouble.

Nine

In principle, the holiday dinner should have been relaxing. Greg liked both Rach's parents. Had from the first time he met them. And today, typically, they were gregarious and easygoing—just comfortable people to be around.

"This is unbelievable." Stan exuberantly sampled the orange-cranberry salad—just before sneaking a wink at Greg. "No one cooks like my daughter."

"Hey," Carolina predictably protested in a wounded voice.

"Now, I love you sweetheart. And you can open a can better than anyone I ever met. But as for cooking—"

Carolina promptly tried sneaking a wink at him, too. "Greg, do I have to sit here and take these insults? Couldn't you punch him for me?"

"Well, I could. If I wanted to risk my life. Personally I think a guy'd have to be insane to try getting between the two of you.'' For two seconds he almost caught Rachel's eye across the table, but she was busy passing the oyster and mushroom stuffing. She'd been busy nonstop since they got here. Too busy. She looked like an adorable wood sprite in her forest-green sweater and playful gold-and-green earrings, but her smiles couldn't fool a lover. She was being ultracareful around her parents, doing the thoughtful daughter and competent hostess thing, but Greg could see she was tense.

Hell, so was he.

Stan was a man's man, had a drawling sense of humor and obviously loved his daughter more than life—which was all it took for Greg to like him. Carolina had a few more crinkles around the eyes than Rach, but it was easy to see where the daughter had inherited the gorgeous blue eyes and sassy figure. Her mom never hesitated to intrude her opinion on anyone or anything, another quality Greg liked. You never had to worry where you stood with Carolina—she'd tell you—and her frequently expressed desire to murder her ex-son-in-law had endeared her to Greg early on.

Being around her parents had never been a cause for tension. Not for him. Yet, as he passed the turkey plate—and some laughing comment with it—he could feel his mood dropping lower than a well pit. In theory, a guy should have been happy he got on so well with his best girl's parents. Instead he felt as depressed as a glum gargoyle.

The problem was, he'd always been the kind of man that parents went for. Stable. Sturdy. Responsible. And all the rest of that type of Boy Scout yadda yadda. The exact opposite of a woman's fantasy for a dynamite or exciting lover.

Again he tried to catch Rachel's eye, but her mom diverted him with another of her personal grilling questions. "I'll bet you miss your family on a holiday like this, don't you?"

"Yes, but they'll be up here for Christmas, and my brother will also fly in from Japan. Everyone lives too far these days to connect for every holiday, but we have a great time when we do. This year, though, I'm just as glad to be home. I'd hate to have missed Rach's pecan pie and whatever she does to those sweet potatoes to make him taste like candy."

Greg could see Carolina look at her daughter. *A family man. And someone who appreciates you besides. How come you two can't be more than friends?* And wanted to cringe. But then her mom was peering at him again with that darling smile—and more nosy probing.

"Rachel mentioned more than once what a terrible car accident you had been through. You feel completely okay now?" Stan suddenly glanced up with a studying look at him, too.

"Couldn't be better. Still have a little weakness in my right arm, and my ribs still squeak some if I laugh too hard. But everything else is fine."

Carolina passed her plate to her husband as if he were expected to mind read whether she wanted more corn bread or more salad. "You look so different, Greg. I almost didn't recognize you when we first walked in. Does it hurt? Your face?"

"No, not really. Sometimes the jaw feels a little tender. Or just...tender." It hadn't gone away, the feeling that he was walking around in someone else's face. And two nights before, he'd wakened in a cold sweat, a nightmare where Rachel peeled off the mask he was wearing and discovered he was still only Greg Stoner. But most of that was just the goofiness of dreams and had nothing to do with Carolina's questions. "I'm basically completely healed. But for a few months I'd just as soon no one punch me in the nose," he said dryly.

Carolina smiled warmly. "I hardly think you're the kind of man to invite anyone doing that kind of thing."

She meant something complimentary, but all Greg could think was no, he wasn't the kind to invite a physical confrontation. Rachel's parents had always had him pegged correctly. He was no fighter, no swashbuckler, no hero. He'd always been the kind of man who argued with words. How dull could you get?

Eventually the group groaned about how they stuffed they were, and then the men kicked the women out of the kitchen to do the cleanup. Stan switched on the microsize TV in the corner to a football game while Greg started filling the sink. With his wife out of sight, Stan lit up a cigar, and the two men alternately chatted and swore—depending on what team was scoring in the game.

Greg's mind, though, was on nothing but Rach. Since last Saturday he'd been trying to believe that their making love was a good thing. Good for her. It wasn't really about sex. It was about helping Rach win her sexual confidence back, and judging from her increasingly creative and dangerous ideas when the lights went out, Greg figured she surely couldn't need to worry about that confidence thing for the next five or six centuries. Soonest.

That whole justification for sleeping with her had sounded so convincingly winning to his conscience.

Only, that walnut just wouldn't crack.

He wanted her. More than his life. He was crazy in love with her, as if a velvet vise were wrapped around his heart.

But this dinner and especially the conversation about his changed appearance had reminded him of the same old problems he'd tried to forget. Rach's desire for him had only shown up after he got a new face. A good-looking, princelike face. And Greg liked wearing the prince's shoes. He'd *be* that prince for her—if he could.

Only, the frog was still down there, just under the surface. Her parents recognized him for the responsible, good-guy dork he was. And he was a good man, for God's sake. Just not an exciting man. Not…hot, sexy, dynamic, mysterious, the kind of guy to inspire a woman to fall hard and deeply. Rachel loved him the way someone loved butter brickle ice cream and a warm fire on a cold night. Love. Not *love*.

He'd already lost his heart, but he didn't want to risk losing Rach from his life completely, and he could well do that if she knew how he really felt. Helping her was okay. Embroiling himself too deeply in her life was not. A frog didn't really metamorphose into a prince—and Greg knew it.

Three nights later, Rachel flipped on the kitchen light around five—the evening was already darker than gloom—and then opened the refrigerator door. Leftovers had dwindled to a couple spoonfuls of vegetables, maybe half a cup of orange-cranberry relish, and, of course, five million pounds of turkey.

Could she face another turkey sandwich?

When the choice was cooking and dishes, versus another no-work meal, the answer was obvious. She loaded her arms with the sandwich ingredients, nudged the fridge door closed with her hip and aimed for the sink counter. Instinctively her gaze shot up when lights suddenly switched on in Stoner's kitchen. She identified a certain unmistakable small, flat guy-fanny—bending over his open refrigerator door.

She started tapping her foot. Fretfully. She munched on a bite of turkey, then a bite of lettuce, skipping the sandwich-making altogether.

Outside, a fresh foot of snow glazed the yards like marshmallow frosting on a fresh-made cake, glazey, shining under a sky seasoned heavily with stars. He was eating alone. She was eating alone.

He glanced up, waved cheerfully.

She cheerfully waved right back…then tapped her foot again. They'd been eating alone. And sleeping alone. Since Thanksgiving Day. Of course, her parents—much as she loved them—could have kiboshed the most ardent lover's mood on Thursday. And she'd disappeared most of yesterday, because it would have been blasphemous not to shop for Christmas the day after Thanksgiving. But that just didn't exactly explain why they were suddenly sleeping alone, when all last week they'd been inseparable.

Her mom once said that loving a man meant loving his cold feet, too.

Rachel understood—perfectly—how easily it was to get emotional cold feet, when she had them herself. The last thing on the planet she wanted to do was confront him. Why would she want to risk hearing that he didn't want to be around her anymore? That his intimate interest in her had already petered out? That she'd talked herself— again—into believing that a man loved her, when reality seemed more like she could play the starring role in the most throw-outable woman since the beginning of time.

No. She definitely didn't want to confront Stoner and risk hearing any version of that soul-slicing hurt. But tarnation. She couldn't keep living in a limbo of trying to guess why the Sam Hill he was making a lone dinner in his kitchen while she was making a lone dinner in hers.

On impulse she spun around. Her eyes narrowed on the

basement door. Seconds later, she flew down the dusty steps, negotiated a petrifying cobweb and opened the fuse box. She turned a fuse. Just a little.

Easy as that, the whole house went black.

Swiftly she closed the fuse box and, groping in the dark, chased back up the stairs in her stocking feet, closed the basement door and peered out her kitchen window into Greg's.

One minute passed. Then two. Right when he had his hands around a monster-size sandwich, he seemed to absently glance up, and then disappear from her sight...but a millisecond later, he backed up to his kitchen window again. Frowning now. Staring intently at her dark house.

Rachel had ample time to brush her hair, put on lipstick and have her trusty baby-pink flashlight—a gift from her dad—switched on when she answered the pounding on her back door.

"Oh, you darling," she said warmly, "I should have guessed you'd notice it was dark over here and come over. But it's okay. I figure it has to be a fuse? And you showed me how to do those a couple times before. If you were just making dinner—"

"I was. But it was just a sandwich and I already wolfed it down." He stepped in, bringing a blast of Arctic air with him. But once he closed the door, her kitchen suddenly seemed darker and more intimate than the midnight hour under the covers with a lover. Of course Stoner's eyes reflected more heat than a blast furnace, so that may have been the reason.

"Well, I still hate to bother you. You were so good about explaining the fuse thing to me before, and I'm almost positive I can handle it this time—"

"I'll bet you can, too. But like my dad used to put it, it's colder than a witch's tit in a brass bra out here, and just in case your heat is affected by the loss of power, we need to know for sure. We'll just both go down to the basement and take a look, okay?''

"It's okay. I just hate to ask you. You've helped me so many other times—"

That earned her an affectionate cuff on the neck, and then cold lips came down to claim hers, softly, winsomely, scolding her for all the protests. "Shut up, Rach,'' he murmured. "You know damn well I love playing hero, so quit giving me a hard time.''

"Okay.'' The instant she agreed, she got another kiss, this one lingering a whole wicked second longer. Then he was shifting away, hiking toward her basement door and yanking a flashlight from his jacket pocket. "I'll go down first, okay? But you see if you can evaluate the problem, and I'll try and shut up unless I think you need some advice.''

"Sounds good to me.'' He hurled his coat on her kitchen table, then led the way down, his boots clattering on the wooden steps. She demurely followed just behind. "The electricity seems to be out in the whole house, not just one room or two. So I'm supposed to check the fuse box on the right, right?''

"Not exactly, sweet pea. The box on the right has all the individual circuits. The left box has all the big power switches, remember?''

"Oh. Yeah. Now I do....'' She made out like it was tough to open the fuse box lid and hold the flashlight at the same time, trying to stall. So far, this venture was going dismally. Stoner was going to figure out her fuse problem in about two seconds, and then how was she going to keep him there? Turtle-slow, she aimed her flashlight beam in every direction but the problem. "Greg, I really haven't had the chance to thank you. You were terrific with my parents on Thanksgiving.''

"I'm the one who owed you the thanks for asking me to that terrific feast. And your parents are no challenge to be nice to. They're both great people.''

A gentle guiding palm under her elbow forced her dratted flashlight beam right on the fuse that was twisted a tad squee-jawed. *Next* time she sabotaged something, she'd try harder to do it right. "Well, I love them, too, but I was still worried they'd guess we were, um…''

"Sleeping together?'' Without skipping a beat, he murmured, "Now just step a little closer. Close enough to sense—without touching—if any of those fuses are particularly hot. Remember what I told you about safety?''

"Uh-huh. But nothing feels hot. Or looks weird. And on the family, I just didn't want you put in an uncomfortable position—''

"Rachel.'' Suddenly his voice was as cool as hoarfrost. "You never had to worry that I would let on our sleeping arrangements to your parents. I could guess you didn't want them to know.''

"Huh?'' She blinked, feeling confused both by his words and sharp tone. She tried to whip the flashlight beam around so she could see his face—surely she hadn't hurt his feelings? But he diverted the yellow stream of light back toward the fuse box. "I only didn't want them to know for your sake,'' she said clearly. "My mom would have hounded you to death with less-than-subtle questions. And my dad can get as bad on the matchmaking routine as she can.''

"Uh-huh. All right, now, test to see if each fuse is screwed in securely.''

"Okay. I'm doing that right now. Greg—''

"The matchmaking thing wouldn't have bothered me

anyway. I've been through it before. Parents have a habit of looking at me as if I were a saintlike possibility for their daughters.''

She glanced at him. He made those words sound like an insult to himself instead of a compliment. ''You sure don't sound happy about that.''

''Nothing to be happy or unhappy about. It's just a fact. Parents look at me and think aha, there's a nice sedate settled guy. Women look and think I'm the kind of man who'd make a decent friend.''

Again, he wasn't saying anything bad about himself. But his tone made it sound that way. And Rachel kept getting the impression he was trying to underline something loud and clear for her.

''Rach!''

''What?'' In the dusty, cobwebbed basement with the gloom only lightened by a couple of flashlights, it wasn't like she could see his expression clearly.

''I'm pretty sure you'd like some light and power some time before the twenty-second century? We're here to check fuses, remember?''

''I am, I am!'' She whisked around, fingering and fussing and trying to look serious about the fuse problem. ''Well, for heaven's sake...''

''What?''

''I think I found the devil.'' Slowly she tightened the offending culprit, and naturally, lights promptly sprang on everywhere, as did a noisy cacophony of hot water heaters and furnaces and refrigerator motors. ''Aha, and you didn't think a woman could handle this, now did you, Stoner?''

''Are you kidding? I never doubted you for a second. Give or take.'' His tone had turned more naturally teasing, but he was frowning. ''I sure don't understand how a fuse

could loosen up like that, though. Maybe it's going bad.
I don't want you without juice in winter temps like this.
I'm going to take a closer look, okay?''

"Sure.'' It was easy to be as obedient as an eighteenth-
century mistress now. If she never saw another fuse in
five centuries, it'd be too soon. "While you're still messing around, I'll head up to the kitchen and make some
Irish coffee. Warm us both up on a cold night like this.''

Before he could say no, she whisked upstairs. Moments
later, she'd started a fresh pot of coffee and began an
exploring mission in the fridge for the whipped cream.
Mentally, though, she struggled to understand Stoner's behavior. He was putting himself down again. Making subtle
little deprecating comments that were supposed to be
funny. And that hurt—because she'd hoped their making
love would help change that negative self-image he had.
She wanted him to feel fabulous about himself as a man—
the way he made her feel as a woman.

Instead, their new sexual relationship seemed to affect
him on a par with...oh, say, a sunshiny day. Nice. Nothing earth-shattering or life shaking, but nice.

If she didn't love the damn man, she'd have been
mightily tempted to shoot him. That not being an option,
she poured an extragenerous dose of whiskey in the coffee
mug going to him. And violently whipped the cream.

Stoner climbed the stairs just as she'd finished prepar-
ing the two mugs. "That looks great.'' Yet he sighed and
scraped a frustrated hand through his hair. "I'm afraid I
couldn't find anything wrong with the fuse. I changed it,
put in a new one. But it just didn't make any sense. The
fuse didn't look old or corroded—nothing.''

"I can't imagine what happened,'' Rachel said, and
then swiftly, "Try the coffee.''

He inhaled a gulp, then grinned. "Whew. That's a potent brew. Who'd guess a nondrinker like you would come up with this one,'' he teased.

"It's my dad's recipe. You think it's too strong?''

"I think it'll put hair on my chest.''

"Well, it better not put any on mine.'' She took a small sip, motioning him toward the living room and the more comfortable chairs, but he leaned against the counter.

"I'll visit for a minute, but I really need to hightail it home after this, Rach. I'm in the middle of a work project.''

"No sweat, I understand,'' she said cheerfully, but it *was* a sweat. A heart-tearing, aching-hurt kind of sweat. Something was motivating him to keep a distance. And if he didn't love her, then he didn't, but there didn't seem a *reason* to rip out her soul. They'd been getting along like lovers on fire, coming home from their respective jobs to fall on each other, using lovemaking as an hors d'oeuvre, appetizer and dessert on a daily basis until Thanksgiving Day. Nothing had happened, nothing said, to account for his sudden physically avoiding her.

She sipped at her Irish coffee, leaning against the opposite kitchen counter—giving him all the blasted physical distance he could want—but she studied him under the hard kitchen light, as objectively and judgmentally as she possibly could. His dark hair still glistened from snow, shagging past his collar, sweeping on one side of his brow. His cheeks were still ruddy from the night cold. His jeans fit loose over long, lean thighs, and the long-sleeved black tee made his shoulders look beam-broad. The whole picture was gorgeous. Sexy. Strikingly male and formidably adorable these days. There were no tips in his appearance—not one—to make anyone think Greg Stoner needed anyone to worry about him.

But she *was* worried. The thing was, Stoner hid his

secrets even better than a priest. Nobody knew he had a
wounded side. Neighbors, family, his co-workers—everyone admired him, liked him. He was good at so many
things, calm in a crisis, competent, someone everyone
trusted and liked being with. No one seemed to realize
he'd guarded painful feelings about himself as a dork or
a nerd. Except for her. Which meant if she didn't do
something about it, just maybe, no one would.

"So..." She waved her mug at him, friendly fashion.
"What was your worst nightmare?"

"Huh?"

The question, of course, hit him out of the blue. But
short of using a cattle prod, Rachel didn't know how else
to force him to talk about himself. "Didn't you have
nightmares as a kid? I sure did."

"Well, yeah. Of course. But I don't know as I remember any."

"Not even one? No recurring dreams of any kind?"

He scratched his chin. "Well...I vaguely remember
parts of an old nightmare. I used to be an A student, but
I couldn't spell worth beans. Even so, the school always
put me in the spelling contest—as if you're smart in math
and science, you must inherently be smart in other sub-
jects, too? Anyway, in this dream, I get up and spell some
real simple word wrong that everyone else knows, and
they're all laughing at me." He shrugged. "That's it. Not
too exciting, huh?"

So typically, he related the dream as if it were a no-
count, foolish story. Yet her heart hurt, just imagining the
young boy in that humiliating situation. And as if a puzzle
piece suddenly clicked into place, Rachel suddenly understood why Stoner'd worked hard at looking nondescript and invisible for so long. He was so bright, but that
IQ thing had made him feel alone and isolated from his

peers as a kid. Turning into someone who faded in the woodwork was so much safer emotionally.

"I think that's what love is," she said thoughtfully. "In part anyway. Being with someone you trust. Who you know would never humiliate you. Even on those days you fail a spelling test—so to speak."

He chuckled, but then took another long slug of Irish coffee, his gaze intent on her face. "So…if for some God unknown reason we're talking about old nightmares…it's your turn. What was your toughest dream as a kid?"

Hmmph. He'd neatly deflected the conversation away from himself—again—but Rachel still answered him, because at least it was keeping him here and talking. "Well…I used to have this one regular nightmare over and over. Someone's chasing me in the dark, and I'm petrified, running through the neighborhood, trying to escape this guy, screaming for help. All I need is for someone to open the door and let me in—and I have every reason to think this will happen because I know everyone, they're all neighbors and friends. But the twist that makes this dream a nightmare is that I have no voice—so I'm screaming and screaming but no one can hear me."

Greg winced. "Yikes. That's a mean one." He hesitated. "You know what that dream makes me think of?"

"What?"

"I don't know if you had that dream when you were married, but it sounds like that was how you felt with your ex-husband. Like you had needs and feelings, but he wouldn't hear you. Or didn't give enough of a damn to listen."

She nodded wryly. "You've got that right. I just wish it hadn't taken me so long to get out of that relationship."

Again his eyes met hers with an odd intensity. "These

last few months, you really have put him behind you. It's different, isn't it?''

''Yeah, it is.'' It was her turn to hesitate. ''Everyone wanted me to divorce him sooner, Greg. Everybody thought I was stupid for staying as long as I did. But as hokey as it sounds, I believe in the marriage vows. I believe in working through the rough parts. I believe in marriage. So I stayed—probably longer than I should have—because I needed to be sure on the inside that I'd done everything I could do to make the marriage work. The bimbo was the last straw. But maybe I did wait too long, because I walked out the door with absolutely no self-confidence left.''

''I understand. And it always made sense to me why you shut off from dating for a long time. Living alone was self-protection. Why would you willingly risk getting hurt again before you'd had a chance to heal...? But you're feeling good about opening those doors again, aren't you?''

She tilted her head, facing his eyes frankly. ''Yes.''

He finished the last of his Irish coffee and plunked the mug on the counter. ''I've been looking for an excuse to say this to you for a while—it just felt awkward, and I'm no good with talking about emotional stuff. But...I'm glad—and honored—you first opened the door first with me. I know you trust me as a friend. But I don't want you ever worried that I'd assume something about the two of us that you don't mean. You're coming back to life after a long hiatus. It feels good. I hope it's good for you in every way. But if you start to feel stronger, I promise I'll understand.''

For a few stunned seconds Rachel stared at him. Her heart seemed to have climbed up somewhere in her throat and stalled there. ''Stoner...you think I'm using you?

That I'd sleep with you as if you were a medicine for my old hurts and insecurities?''

''No. Hell. I knew I wouldn't say that right.'' Edgily Greg shifted on his feet. ''I never thought you were using me in any selfish or manipulative way. Ever. I was just trying to say that I understand—''

He understood nothing, Rachel thought furiously. My God. They were back at square one. Stoner just refused to acknowledge the idea that she just might be hopelessly, helplessly, wonderfully in love with him. How could they possibly have come this far if Greg was still locked up on the same old problem? He *loved*. He just couldn't seem to believe that anyone could love *him*.

Rachel wanted to cry. Or claw out her hair. But she could hardly stand there and lose the best man she'd ever known—or ever dreamed of loving—because he was a blockheaded blindsided dunderhead. Obviously she had to do something.

Ten

Rachel charged across the kitchen, surged up on her tip-toes and yanked on his ears. She remembered yanking Stoner down to her height to kiss him before. She remembered being just this furious with him before. And she deeply remembered the humiliation of sleeping with a man who didn't need her before.

But damnation. Greg wasn't her jerkwater ex. She hadn't known how fiercely and completely a woman could love a man until him, and they couldn't keep going on this way. Stoner had been putting himself down. Again. And she simply couldn't give up this wondrous man, this hero of her heart, without fighting for him at least one more time.

So she spanked her lips against his, stinging hard, communicating with precise clarity how royally ticked off she was.

Only, almost instantly Greg started melting on her.

Gentling hands kneaded her shoulders under her old, gnarly yellow mohair sweater, and then his palms glided down her arms in a soothing, quieting caress. He never stopped the kiss. He never lost the connection. But he responded to her fury with tenderness and loving warmth.

It was darn hard to hold on to her temper, but she jerked her mouth free. "Stoner—do you know why I made love with you?"

"Something tells me any way I answer that question is going to get me in trouble."

She suspected he wanted to lighten the moment, to make her smile. Instead she yanked the cord on the light over the sink. She didn't want him distracted by the yellow counters or the old cracked linoleum, or the blinger-cold light glaring in his eyes. "You're right. Because if you don't give me the right answer, you'll not only be in big trouble...but you could really hurt me, Stoner. That question is no joke to me."

She saw something in those gorgeous blue eyes—fear? Dread? Yet the pad of his thumb gently smoothed a lock of hair from her cheek. "All right," he said softly. "You want honesty, Rach, and I don't ever want to give you less. I think you made love to me because you were over the creep and ready to get on with your life in every way. But sex was still a land mine. Sex is always a land mine. And you wanted—needed—to get your sexual feet wet after all this time with someone safe, comfortable. Someone you knew positively that you could trust."

"*Wrong.*" Hells bells, the idiot man forced her to kiss him again. She hated that look of anxiety in his eyes, hated him worrying about hurting her. Her mouth smoothed his, soothed his, then latched on with simmering, shimmering pressure. She reached up, with infinite care touched the new, strong line of his jaw, pushed up, sieved into the wiry texture of his thick hair. Her heart was suddenly pounding, pounding against the hard wall of his chest. But sooner or later she had to surface for air. And so did he.

"Wrong? Are you saying you don't trust me, Rach?"

"Of course, I trust you, you blitz-brain. I also trust my banker—but I wouldn't sleep with him if my life depended on it. So try for another answer or risk the consequences."

"Because you didn't want to be with a stranger. Because you feel safe with me."

"Wrong. Dead wrong. Again." Clearly she hadn't threatened him with specific consequences before. Her hands yanked the black tee free from his jeans, found hot skin beneath, found ribs, found muscles tensing and pulsing under her slightest touch. She wound her arms around his back, then down, felt his sinewy little butt flex under the pressure of her splayed palms. Faster than a streak of lightning, his arousal was suddenly ironed neatly, precisely between them. And his gaze expressed shock—she was afraid he was shocked at her brazenness. Instead it seemed to be hurt flashing in his eyes.

"Rachel? You really don't feel safe with me?"

"*Yes,* I feel safe with you, you dolt. I'd feel safe in the company of a cop or priest, too—but you think I'd sleep with them? Come on, Stoner. This question just isn't that hard. And you're running out of time to get the answer right." Her fingers discovered the snap on his jeans. Then located his fly.

His eyes suddenly looked murky, glazed. Or possibly her vision was affected by a sudden intense dizziness. Her fingers seemed to have triggered something that was already swollen and fully charged. And his mouth was responsible for her loss of equilibrium.

"I hate to tell you this, Rach, but I've completely forgotten the question," he said thickly. And then swooped down.

The kiss came at her like a bird of prey. Smooth. Elegant. Powerful. And in response, her blood pressure suffered a vivid surge and her heartbeat sang with a delicious sensation of excitement. Her head reeled back. The taste of him short- circuited all the neuron paths to her defenses. He took that first kiss. And then he took another three.

She thought if he were going to react this violently, maybe she'd better ask his permission before touching his fly next time.

Or maybe not.

She had his pants opened and loosened—but not down—when Stoner suddenly rucked up her fuzzy yellow sweater. Lifted his mouth. Zipped the sweater over her head at rocket speeds. Then came back to kiss her again.

Cool, drafty air shivered over her bared skin. They were in the kitchen, she reminded herself from somewhere inside a ditsy, delirious fog. Surely nothing was going to happen in the kitchen.

Or maybe it was.

His hands streaked down her spine, leaving a foggy white vapor trail of sensation, and then his palms cupped bottom and lifted her. She knew they weren't dancing—she knew—yet the room was suddenly spinning around in the wildest of waltzes. Somehow he managed to shimmy off her old gray cords before setting her fanny on the edge of the kitchen table. And while his hands were busy, hers took advantage by pushing his jeans down a little farther. Just a little farther. Enough.

She desperately wanted to touch him, but he kept distracting her. He refused to stop kissing her in that dizzying way, teeth nipping at teeth, his tongue conspiring with her tongue, tastes mingling and whispering with each other. Her breath kept coming in stolen gasps. His kept coming in groans.

Her oak-door kitchen table was heaped with mail and pencils and napkins and colorful place mats. For a second or two. His arm swept everything off, and before she even heard the thumps and clatters of debris falling on the floor, his fingers were pinching the snap of her bra. Chilly drafts raised gooseflesh on her bare skin. For a second or two.

His mouth homed down, skipping her lips this time, grazing a nibbling path under her jaw, down her throat, down to nestle and nuzzle at her breasts. Then feast.

And to think she'd been so desperately worried about his lack of self-confidence.

The flat table surface felt cold and uncomfortable on her spine—until her legs bicycled up and wrapped around his waist. His mouth shifted, twisted, branding silver-soft kisses up her neck, on the raging pulse beat of her throat. She felt his bare abdomen against her bare abdomen. The mobile, supple give of his flesh, the heat of his skin, his lustrous black hair shivering between her fingers. She took all those wild, hard, possessive kisses he'd been stealing from her and stole 'em all back.

Her heart was pounding, pounding, her lungs complaining they could only catch oxygen in slices. Too bad. She wasn't wasting time breathing when anything was this good, this rich, this beyond anything she knew. And she had known desire before. But nothing like this. He'd stirred every one of her hormones blissfully awake before. More than once. But not like this. Lust was the difference. She loved him, differently, more dangerously, more vulnerably, than she ever guessed love could be. Who'd have guessed that love could bring on a disgraceful, wicked case of lust like this?

Desire reeled her to him on a sharp hook. She just wanted to taste his shoulder. Take a little bite from his neck. Gently smooth and soothe caresses around his ribs, because she was always afraid of hurting him there, but he wasn't going to miss a little wedge out of his collarbone, now was he?

His groan sounded like he'd swallowed a throat full of gravel. ''You're sure you want to play this down and dirty, Rach?''

''Uh-huh.''

''More comfortable upstairs. And before this goes any further, I could get you upstairs.'' He reconsidered that swiftly made promise. ''I think.''

''Don't think. I don't want you to think. I want you inside me. Now.''

There now. He lost it. The eyes changed from gorgeous blue to a turbulently stormy blue, vivid, glazey. He filled his hands with her breasts, then bent down to suckle and nuzzle the soft white skin with the scratchy stubble on his cheeks. He took a nip—without permission. Hard enough to leave a mark the next day. Hard enough to make her legs tighten around him and her hands clutch and pull.

''I love you,'' she whispered. ''You have no idea how much.''

''I think I loved you before I met you. Dreamed of you before I knew you.''

His words touched her, but the passion and yearning need in his voice ignited her heart far more. His lips and hands, teeth and tongue, sashayed from her breasts down her torso, then streaked a new path back up again. His mouth felt lush, his tongue soft, each kiss compelling another and another. The drafty kitchen heated hotter than a furnace. Snow cuddling in the windowsills tried to melt. The harsh ceiling light blurred into rainbows. And as desire whiplashed through her—sharp now, not fun, fierce and desperate now, not just playing—still, hope circled her mind on loving wings.

She wanted a life with Greg. She wanted everything—life, love, babies, passion so wild it blew them both out of the water. And if she had to lay her heart bare-naked and vulnerable, it was always worth that risk if it compelled Greg to see what they could be together, for each other.

And tonight, for the first time, she felt her heart-fears seep away, because he surely was trying to share exactly the same thing with her.

His mouth nipped and laved and savored every inch of skin up to her lips, and by the time his face hovered over hers, her eyes were open. So were his. She could see the tension in his brow, the fire in his eyes. His shoulders had a sheen of damp gold, his unruly hair wild as a warrior's, and his arms held her legs so she could feel his arousal. He was hot, hard, pulsing—alive, seeking a nest for his need—and for hers.

Then he filled her. And they both tipped off the sky and soared into each other.

It was a good two hours later before she felt recovered, and by then they'd moved upstairs to her bedroom. Her fuzzy-screened ten-inch TV provided just enough illumination so they wouldn't spill their marshmallow sundaes. Stoner was as starved as she was, not because they'd both missed dinner but because—he claimed—she'd forced him to work off so many calories.

"You're blaming me for our disgraceful decadent behavior on the kitchen table?"

"Well, sheesh, Rach. There are only two of us. You can't expect me to take responsibility, can you?"

She chortled as she set her empty sundae dish on the tray on the floor. He'd leveled his just a few minutes earlier. "What beats me is what on earth we're doing in this room."

"Gaining strength so we can make love again?"

Her cheeks flushed. "I meant…what we're doing in *my* bedroom, rather than yours. You have the water bed. The five-inch-thick carpeting. The big screen tube."

"Yeah…but you let me eat stuff in your bed."

"Excuse me? Are you trying to say you wouldn't let us have crackers or potato chips or a sundae if we were in your bed?"

"Of course we could. I just didn't know that until we slept over here. I thought it was in the rule book. No potato chips in bed."

"It is."

"Yeah, but in your bed, I got the idea that I could just lick 'em off your chest. There's something different about my bedroom. I've slept alone there for years and those kinds of ideas never occurred to me."

Well, then, she felt compelled to kiss him. And then he seemed compelled to kiss her back. After which they resumed their silly talk all over again. Lovers' talk, the kind of talking where she smiled over nothing and so did he, and no one could have made sense of the conversation except them. Whatever flashed motion and color on the TV screen was welcomed for the light, but neither noticed nor cared what shows were being aired.

Pillows were piled high behind them both, the hour so late, all the traffic sounds outside had completely died. The snow kept coming, quieter now, softer, hitting the windows in sudden little splotches of froth, white lace frost rimming the edges. He'd hogged most of the comforter, which Rachel had first chuckled about.

It was only now that a bee-bite awareness started to gnaw on her mind. Old-fashioned radiators poured out heat in her bedroom, too much so. Propped on the pillow right next to him, she could see Greg's glossy tumbled hair. The gleam in his eyes. The smile that regularly teased the corner of his mouth. But where she was warm enough in just a sheet, he'd covered up his whole body with the comforter.

And that gradually started to trouble her. Maybe Greg was a modest man. Why should it only be women who had those kinds of feelings? Only, heaven knew, he'd shown no modesty anytime he ever had his arms around her. But that's specifically what started to worry her. It was only after they'd made love that he'd yanked up that comforter. Right then. He didn't want her to see him? Physically? After everything they'd shared?

Across the room, a wavy mirror hung over her early-attic dresser. ''You see us over there?'' she murmured to him.

He never bothered glancing at the mirror. He seemed to be looking at her. Savoring her with his eyes. Loving every part of her that he could see. ''I see you of the Meg Ryan eyes and the wild blond hair and the, oops, tip of marshmallow at the corner of her mouth.'' Which he promptly and helpfully licked off for her.

Her blood stirred, thickened. Let sleeping dogs lie, she warned herself...but before that unforgettable episode on the kitchen table, she'd been warning herself of the exact opposite. She'd let too many sleeping dogs lie where Greg was concerned. ''I wanted you to see the guy lying next to me in the mirror,'' she teased lightly.

''Oh. Him.'' He glanced at the mirror, playing the game

for her. But only for a nanosecond. And in that nanosecond, she saw his shoulders suddenly hunch, had the impression that smile looked glued on instead of real.

"Greg?"

"What?"

"It bugs you to look at yourself in the mirror?"

"No. Of course not. How could a guy live without mirrors? We'd kill ourselves shaving."

"But..." she coaxed him.

"But...hell, I admit it. Even all these weeks since the surgery, I feel like I'm looking at a stranger instead of myself. And it makes me uncomfortable."

"Come on. Just because you got a new jaw? And lost some weight?"

"No." He swallowed. Stared up at the ceiling, then back at her. The humor in his expression disappeared, but the honesty in his eyes was suddenly real and raw. "Because I'm afraid you're attracted to me only because I look different."

Hurt stabbed her heart before she could stop it. She'd known there was something wrong. She'd known before they made love. "You think I'm that shallow a person?"

"No, no—"

"You think I care whether you're handsome or not? That I'd judge or love a man based on whether he had a cute tush?"

"No, stop. Don't put words in my mouth, Rach. I swear, that was never what I meant." He let out a breath, struggled to try again and then said slowly, "Most of my life, I was pudgy and overweight. That's how I think of myself. That's who I am. The bumbling, overweight pedantic old nerd—the guy you probably tried to run away from when you were in ninth grade."

"Maybe in ninth grade I happened to like talking to bumbling, pedantic old nerds," she snapped back.

"Come on, Rachel. You're beautiful. In ninth grade you were probably talking to the class president, the class jocks, the leaders in your peer group. And I suspect you were kind to the nerds—I can't imagine you being otherwise—but that doesn't mean you planned on pairing off with one. And yeah, I'm aware that I don't look so dorky or nerdlike now. But you never noticed me—not in a sexual way—until after the plastic surgery. That's just a fact."

Frustration slugged through her pulse. So did fear. All this time she'd known that something troubled Greg about her, about their relationship. And she'd understand they each had their own personal battles with self-confidence. Who didn't? But where Stoner had so wonderfully helped her, she felt at a loss to understand a problem he couldn't seem to openly share with her. Or didn't want to.

She said slowly, carefully, "You're right. That I didn't think of you—sexually—before the accident. But that was partly because I wasn't looking at any man that way, Stoner, until I felt more healed from the divorce. And then we spent all that time together in the hospital. Talk time. Personal time. I just got to know you in a completely different way. But it was never because you looked differently."

"Maybe."

"Not maybe. For sure."

"Rach. I'm not saying that looks matter to you in some superficial way," he said gently. "I'm saying that I'm still the nerdy dork that you never noticed before. Except as a friend. The kind of safe, comfortable friend you felt you could trust. Which you can. And I hope you never stop feeling that way."

How an unforgettably magic night could go so wrong, she couldn't fathom. Earlier, hope had welled in her heart about love, about their future, about babies with his gorgeous blue eyes. She just couldn't imagine his making love with such fierceness and passion and emotion if he felt nothing more than desire. Now that hope deflated like a punctured tire.

She'd been chasing and chasing and chasing him. She knew it. She was the one who'd started the kisses, who'd maneuvered him into situations of closeness. Tonight was the same, when she'd conned him into coming over with her fake fuse problem. But all this time she thought she'd had to make the first moves, because Greg would never push or presume, not knowing how hurt she'd been from the divorce. The only way he could know that she was truly healed and ready to rejoin life was if she showed him.

Only, her worst fear had always been repeating the same humiliating mistake she'd made with Mark—believing someone loved her who didn't.

Suddenly, swiftly, she pulled up the comforter, concealed all the bareness she could and snapped off the remote control. The TV screen flashed off and the room flooded with true darkness. She lay there, feeling tears forming in her eyes she didn't want him to see. Feeling tears form in her throat she didn't want him to hear.

But finally she said what needed to come out. What should have come out weeks before, before she'd risked—and lost—her whole heart. ''I need to tell you something. Earlier tonight, I asked you a question, about why I made love with you. I thought you knew the answer, Stoner. That I'd fallen in love with you. That I'd never have landed in your bed for any other reason. You don't have to feel the same way…but I can't be friends with you. Not like we were before. Either we're going in the same direction—or we're through.''

Eleven

Greg stared at the budget proposal on his desk. His entire life had been in shambles for the last ten days. The disastrous budget should at least have distracted him from the gloom.

He lived for problems like this. Always had. And because it was almost Christmas, this budget needed balance pronto—and the board of directors would be fully justified in having his head. The problem was, Greg didn't care. Put him in front of a guillotine, what was the difference?

The numbers blurred in front of his eyes. He kept remembering the night Rachel had turned her back on him. The cold snow coming down, the shadowy room with all those ice-cream colors, the drifting scent of her perfume, her skin. His desperately wanting to touch her, hold her, say something brilliant to heal the rift between them.

Only, he didn't know else what to say. He'd been truthful with her. And he cared too much—everything had gone too far—for him not to put the core problem on the line. She thought she loved him. Greg believed she did, too. And it was a wonderful kind of love. The way you'd throw your arm affectionately around your best pal next door, knowing he wasn't so cool, that not mattering—a friend was a friend, and true friendships were one of the sacred relationships on earth.

But a lover's relationship was a whole different thing. The only way the frog got the princess to kiss him in the old fairy tale was to bribe her. And just because he'd metamorphosed into a prince in the looks department, he wasn't willing to bribe Rach. Or lie to her. Or try to talk her into believing he was anything but the same old frog he'd always been.

"Greg?" Startled at the sound of his boss's voice, he glanced up. Monica posed in the doorway, carrying a sheath of papers. "I could have guessed you'd have the budget proposal in front of you. Me, too. Somehow we've got to come to grips with this. Could I talk to you about some of the figures on page eight?"

"Sure." His voice expressed as much pep as roadkill. He jammed on a professional smile and tried again. "I'll be glad to. Just tell me what you don't understand."

She hiked in, wearing a pretty typical power suit—purple today—with a swish of silk at the throat and a dangle of gold at her wrists. Instead of plunking down in the chair across from his desk, though, she came around next to him and bent down. Her scarf brushed his arm. Eventually she pushed it back. After flipping through the budget to the pages she wanted, though, she then rested her hand light, deliberately, on his shoulder.

"Right there," she said. "Doesn't that seem awfully high for Purchasing?"

He'd tried—hard—to ignore her nonsense and just get on with his job. But that took patience, and after the last ten days, Greg was out of patience and out of heart both. He'd lost everything. His best friend. His lover. His soul mate. And he'd have done anything for Rachel to make her happy, but how could pretending to be someone he wasn't ever work for either of them? The point being, his boss had picked the wrong moment to squeeze his shoulders with those plum-hued talons of hers. "Yes, I believe that figure is extremely high for Purchasing. And I'll tell you what I suggest doing about that—as soon as you take your hand off my shoulder."

"I beg your pardon?" The hand lifted as if burned.

"Thanks."

She could have left it there, but no, not Monica. Just like Rach had told him, his boss just plain didn't know how to back down. "I don't understand. We've worked together for years now, Greg. Surely you're not uncomfortable with a little gesture of affection from me?"

"I'm not uncomfortable at all. I'm ticked off. There's a difference. I wouldn't touch any woman employee unless it were accidental, and you know better than to do it with me."

Her chin huffed up. Hurt shone in her eyes, as deliberate as the glint of a rhinestone. "I can't believe that you would completely misunderstand—"

"I haven't misunderstood anything. Look, Monica, I like working here and I like working with you, too. But you either quit with the touching business—now, pronto—or I'm giving you my resignation. And I have nothing else to say, unless you actually came in here with some real questions on the budget proposal...."

On the drive home, the freeway was sloshy and slushy and his mood gloomier than the ominously swirling gray snow clouds. Once he'd said his piece, Monica had shut up and shaped up, but she'd never really been on his mind anyway. His boss was just one of those everyday life problems that he hadn't gotten around to handling before.

But nothing in his life had been right without Rach. He'd have done anything for her. Anything. Yet somehow he'd managed to hurt her and he simply had no clues how to fix this wrong he'd caused.

He edged up the streets, seeing kids finish up a snowman under the streetlights, and another group of urchins staging a snowball fight in the road. Because his gaze was peeled so carefully on the children, he didn't first notice that there was a car in Rachel's driveway. A black Taurus. Last year's model. Not a car from the neighborhood, nor one he recognized as a regular visitor of hers.

Her visitors weren't his business, he grimly reminded himself as he parked in his driveway, gathered his topcoat and briefcase. Once inside his house, though, he flicked on the kitchen light and plunked down his case and keys. And right there—hey, it wasn't his fault—was the kitchen window that overlooked hers.

Like a starved cat in a rainstorm, his eyes honed instantly on Rach. Just a look was all he wanted. One look. And she happened to be in her kitchen, wearing that fuzzy yellow sweater he'd forever associate with making love with her...only, something was wrong. She made an oddly tense, edgy gesture with her hand—and then hurled out of his sight.

And that was when Greg saw the man. The guy was standing by her fridge, a beer in his hand. And something about his appearance looked familiar....

Oh, God.

Muscles tensed in Greg's legs and spine. His eyes narrowed. His jaw clamped down tight, painfully tight, and he'd been infinitely careful with his new jaw until now. But the guy in her kitchen was Mark. Sacred Mark, her ex-husband.

Greg remembered seeing photos. Just a few weeks after Rach moved next door, her parents had driven from Madison, carting a carload of stuff. Clothes. Kitchen utensils, personal items, shoes, lamps…photo albums. Rach hadn't given the old pictures more than a glance—not in his sight—but he'd really wanted a look at the guy who'd hurt her so badly, so he'd stolen a good look.

Mark-the-turd was good looking. Curly brown-almost-black hair. Snapping bright eyes. Not a big guy, no real height, but a lady-killer smile, sex appeal and confidence in the way he stood, the way he wore his clothes.

Greg had hated him on sight, and even through the dirty, snow-sludgy window he could clearly—clearly—see it was him on the far side of her kitchen. Sipping beer. Looking as comfortable as if he owned the place, his mouth open and closing—yapping—at Rach.

Greg peeled off his gray-striped suit jacket. Then yanked at the tie choking his neck. But he couldn't force himself to budge from the window. Not even an inch. He told himself it wasn't his business if Sacred Mark came to visit her. It wasn't like the pond scum was breaking any laws. Ex-husbands were allowed to visit ex-wives. No state laws seemed to recognize that sometimes that should be considered cause for a justifiable homicide.

But what if the jerk had finally come to his senses and realized what he'd lost in Rachel? What if he wanted her back? And what if Rachel was so discouraged and angry because he'd screwed up *their* relationship that she actually listened to the dog?

He yanked the tie completely free from his neck, then wadded it up and hurled it.

He had no business going over there. No business even thinking about it. Rachel didn't want to see him again. Leaving her alone was precisely what Greg wanted to do. He'd hurt her once. The last thing he wanted was to risk hurting her again, and certainly not just because he had selfish needs—like the need to be with her until the day he died. Down the pike, Rach would find her prince. The best thing a frog could do for her was just hop out of her way.

He heeled off a loafer. Then started to heel off the other loafer when he suddenly saw her show up in his window view again. She was walking past Sacred Mark...when the creep suddenly reached out, and with a can of beer in his one hand, grabbed her wrist with the other.

Greg's heart started hammering in his chest.

Maybe a frog couldn't transform into a prince. But there was a limit to what even a frog could stand there and tolerate without doing anything.

And this frog had just reached his limit.

Oh, for Pete's sake. Rachel had had a terrible, heart-shredding week. Her stomach was churning from too much anxiety and caffeine, her head thudding from too many nights of lost sleep, her nerves frayed from a knife-sharp feeling of despair that just refused to lighten.

She was just in no mood for Wayne to pull this crap.

"Hey," she said with an attempt at lightness. "Either move your hand or die."

"Come on, Rachel, loosen up. We're not at work now. No reason we can't have a little fun."

She should never have let Wayne Makovich give her a ride home, but hindsight was always so cheap. When her yellow VW had started coughing and choking in the parking lot at work, she knew from experience that only a hospital stay with a mechanic was going to cure the problem. Wayne was a pushy, touchy, pain in the keester— the only one of her engineers that she'd never trust out of eyesight—but at least he'd never pushed the line. At work. Now she saw the gleam in his eyes, felt the pressure of his beefy hand manacling her wrist and just wanted to sigh from exhaustion.

Some days she felt up for a confrontation. Definitely not tonight. She just wanted to dim the lights and curl up and try to get a grasp on this grieving sense of loss. She'd chased Greg. She'd fought for him. There was nothing else she could do unless he himself valued what they had together. But she'd already lectured herself on that refrain over and over again. Her heart still heard the melody they played when they were together. She couldn't stop hearing it and right now couldn't even imagine that happening.

Wayne's dirty-minded little smirk, though, was starting to annoy her. "I said," she repeated carefully, "remove your hand. Now, Wayne. I appreciate the ride home, I really do. But offering you a beer to thank you was all I was offering. Believe it."

"Jeez. You're so tight all the time." The beer can clunked down on the counter, freeing his other hand. His gaze was still roving over her like he'd like to be the brush for her canvas. "You've been divorced for ages, haven't you? How do you know we couldn't have something going together unless you give us a try. And what's a kiss, babe? No big deal, right?"

"Wrong. Cut it out." His right hand clutched her upper arm. "I mean it. Now." She tried to twist away, but his left hand grabbed her other arm. And that stupid grin of his started aiming for her mouth. "Look. We have to work together, so I don't want this to turn unpleasant—"

"Neither do I. So just give us a kiss and it won't. One kiss. That's all, then I'll quit, I promise. God, you can't really be this prissy—"

A lump filled her throat. A sudden sick feeling that didn't want to go down. Wayne wasn't evil or frightening. He was just a jerk, but because he was a jerk this had already turned into an embarrassing, messy situation that neither of them could get out of gracefully now. He yanked her closer and Rachel thought well, hell, that's it. Her knee was raised—and her right hand clenched in a fist to slug the darn fool—when her back door suddenly slammed open.

Wayne's body blocked her view of the new intruder— but not for long. Everything happened so fast. Wayne's mouth dropped open. Then his face squinched up in pain. But he was hauled around and a fist plowed in his stomach before Rachel caught a glimpse of furious blue eyes.

"Stoner? Holy cow, holy moly, holy spit—"

Wayne was trying to bury his face under his elbows. "Rachel, for God's sake, call him off. Who the hell are you, anyway? Rachel—"

"Did he hurt you?" Greg's eyes, blazing soft, on her face.

"No. No, I'm fine. Really, I—"

"There." Wayne's voice reeked belligerence. "She said she was fine—and you're interrupting something that's none of your business. What the hell gives you the right to barge in here—"

"I love her. That's what gives me the right. And a divorce doesn't give you any rights, much less to touch a lady unless you're asked. If I were you, I'd apologize to

her—real nice and real fast—before you hightail it out the
door.''

"Divorce? Divorce? What on earth is this guy talking
about, Rachel?"

In about twenty minutes all the noise had simmered
down. In fact, her kitchen was quieter than a mauso-
leum—except for the sound of cold running water. The
water wasn't really necessary, but after the jerk left, Rachel had taken one look at his knuckles, shrieked and
promptly grabbed his hand and put it under the cold water
flow. Greg figured he'd survive the swollen knuckles. It
wasn't like he planned a new career as a prizefighter.
What was harder to survive was the minutes of silence
still ticking by.

"Are you mad at me?" he ventured finally.

"No." She lifted his hand from the flow of water, studied it, shook her head and then opened her freezer to fetch
some ice cubes.

"Are you okay?"

"No." She hunched down, found a plastic bag and bus-
ied herself filling it with the cubes.

And he heard the "no." But he had no idea what to
do about it. When the engineer guy had left, Greg would
have been happy to disappear into the woodwork at his
house. Permanently. But Rach had slammed the door—
with him on the inside—glared at him with stunning intensity, started swearing and then done the cold-water-on-
his-hand routine. "Um…could you give me a hint what's
on your mind since you don't seem to be feeling too talk-
ative?"

His hand got wrapped in a towel, dried like it was more
fragile than a baby's butt, then nuzzled with the cooling
ice. He could have sworn he'd made a fool out of himself.

In her eyes. And it was his worst nightmare come to life—showing himself to be a dweeb instead of a heroic prince when it mattered, in front of the woman he loved. Only, it was beginning to seem that Rach didn't see it quite that way.

"You fought for me, Stoner," she whispered.

"I thought it was your ex-husband. Mark."

"I realized that when you mentioned the divorce."

"It looked like a photograph I saw of him. The dark hair, the same build, the type of clothes. And it's not like I was spying on you, Rach. But when I glanced through my kitchen window, I swear, it looked like you were struggling. Like he was grabbing you, hurting you."

"Yeah. Exactly."

She said that "exactly" as if it should have been meaningfully in capital letters. Confused, Greg plopped the ice bag on the counter. Maybe his hand still hurt like fire, but he'd had enough being babied. So far he hadn't understood one thing Rach had done or said—except that logically he thought she'd be mad at him. Or embarrassed.

And the way those soft luminous eyes tilted up to his, she seemed to be neither. "Can't you see, Greg? I've tried and tried to tell you that you're a prince. A man who leaps in to help someone else, especially someone he cares about. You're the kind of man who stands up, who does the right thing, who isn't worried about the cost to himself. And you were that kind of man long, long before the plastic surgeon changed your looks."

Now it was his turn to fall silent.

She threw up her hands, spun around and then leaned back against the far counter. A careful distance from him. But the emotion in her eyes, in her face, in her voice was softer and deeper than thick, golden honey. "It was the prince I fell in love with. At the time I fell in love with him, maybe he was overweight. And not quite so striking in looks. But I really didn't notice that because it didn't matter. He was a hero to me. A man who'd helped me heal. Stood by me. Who didn't even know me when he pitched in to help with the mess I'd made of my life, and never even asked for a return. He was kind. And he had a huge heart. He was smart and funny and perceptive...."

He could feel a mortifying brick-red climbing up his throat. "Rach. Don't. You don't need to say all that stuff—"

"Apparently I did need to say it. Long before this. Because you sure weren't understanding it on your own." When he made a move toward her, she put up her hand in a repressive gesture. "Just stay right there. Because we're not going any further unless we get this settled. You hurt me."

"I know. And God, I'm sorry."

"Sorry isn't good enough. You insulted me by implying that I'd fall for a frog, buster. I fell for a no-count bum once. I admit that. But I was way younger and more stupid then, and I paid all the prices for that. I know my own mind now. My own heart. I know what love is—and what I want and need from the man of my heart."

Maybe she wasn't ready to let him hold her. Yet. But she didn't seem to mind his taking slow, sure steps closer to her. Her eyes seemed huge. No tears had fallen, but they were welling in her eyes—she was that upset, and her voice getting just that much more trembly. That was the first he knew he wasn't going next door to sleep. Ever again.

"Rachel, I promise never—ever—to insult you again. I've been in love with you from the first second I laid eyes on you. There was never anyone who touched me like you do. No woman who even came close. I told you I loved you—"

She nodded, then swallowed hard. "In the middle of the night. But I'm not seventeen anymore, so I wasn't sure if those love words were inspired by the heat of the moment—"

"You bet they were," he assured her, and caught the hint, the promise of a smile. She was losing all that hurt stiffness in her shoulders, all that fragile, careful pride in her pale face. Her eyes were still full, but she was seeing him through those almost-tears now.

"Darn it, Greg, that heat was inspiring to me, too," she admitted wryly. "But I wasn't sure if you meant love…or passion. Or the love of a friend. I knew you loved me as a friend—"

"You're damn right I did. And do. That was part of the problem. I cherished you as a friend, Rach. And if I couldn't have you for a lover, for a wife, then I didn't want to lose you as a friend, too. You're so vibrant and beautiful and full of life, I just—"

"Stoner, if you even *try* saying that you were afraid of boring me, I'm going to kill you. I mean it. I'm going to murder you with my bare hands. And don't you come any closer, either."

But he'd already come closer. Close enough to brush an unruly lock of hair away from her brow. Close enough to thumb-kiss her lower lip in a gesture of tenderness. Close enough to be there, right there, if one of those tears dared fall. "Okay," he said in his best obedient, conciliatory tone. "I won't call myself staid or boring ever again if it bugs you. It's not a problem anyway. As long as you know the truth of who I am."

"I know the truth. You're the most dangerous man I've ever known." One slim hand wrapped around his neck.

Then the other. And suddenly that soft, trembly voice was coming across as both fierce and bossy. "Maybe you're practical and responsible, Stoner. But not when we kiss. If you just kiss me—once—I can show you what I mean."

He cocked his head and brought his smile within a heart's breath of hers. Then kissed her, since she'd asked for it. He took his time, confessing a soul full of dreams and hopes with that kiss. He talked to her about raising kids in the old family Victorian house, girls with her adorable perky smile and Meg Ryan eyes, boys with annoying ultrabrains who worried way too much about their nerdlike personalities. He promised her long nights, cuddling up on the back porch swing, making wild love on the kitchen table, growing old together, growing young together. Growing. Together. And he had more things he wanted to communicate with that kiss, but about then he needed to surface for air. So did she.

"See?" Rach whispered breathlessly.

What he *saw* was a lady asking for trouble with those huge blue eyes. And he was about to give her a lifetime of trouble—whatever it took to make her happy—but then she started talking again.

"You asked me more than once if I felt safe with you. And I lied and told you yes. But the real heart answer is no. I feel wild. I feel reckless. I feel a hundred times more sexy and beautiful and desirable than I really am. And I love those dangerous feelings—"

"So do I." If they were going to marry, Greg figured he'd better start finishing her sentences for her. "And all those dangerous feelings come from loving you. From who you are as a lover, Rach. And from who we are together."

"Finally," she whispered. "I was so afraid I'd lost you. That you didn't care as much as I did."

"I couldn't love you more. Sometimes I think you cast a spell on me before I even knew you...the one woman who could make all the difference in my life, who opened up my world and everything I once knew about love." Hell, she was the one who was good at this talking business. Not him. So he quit trying and reached for her again, thinking that he'd experiment with spells and kisses that swept her away and love that richened her life—the way she'd richened his.

*   *   *   *   *

Look for Jennifer Greene next in a special
MONTANA MAVERICKS *Collection coming to bookstores in March 2000. And be sure to watch for more of Jennifer Greene's stories in Silhouette Desire...soon!*

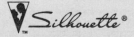

If you enjoyed what you just read,
then we've got an offer you can't resist!

Take 2 bestselling love stories FREE!

Plus get a FREE surprise gift!

*Membership in this family has
its privileges…and its price.
But what a fortune can't buy,
a true-bred Texas love is sure to bring!*

Coming in November 1999…

Expecting…
In Texas
by

MARIE
FERRARELLA

Wrangler Cruz Perez's night of passion with Savannah Clark
had left the beauty pregnant with his child. Cruz's cowboy
code of honor demanded he do right by the expectant
mother, but could he convince Savannah—and himself—
that his offer of marriage was inspired by true love?

THE FORTUNES OF TEXAS continues with
A Willing Wife by Jackie Merritt,
available in December 1999 from
Silhouette Books.

Available at your favorite retail outlet.

SILHOUETTE®
Desire

COMING NEXT MONTH

#1249 HEART OF TEXAS—Mary Lynn Baxter
Man of the Month 10th Anniversary
Businessman Clark Garrison had come home to River Oaks for
one purpose—to make a profit. But that was before he met
Dr. Sara Wilson...and realized his profit would be her loss.
Would Sara still want to be his partner in life once the truth
was revealed?

#1250 SECRET AGENT DAD—Metsy Hingle
Texas Cattleman's Club
Widow Josie Walter had never wanted to get close to another
man again, but she couldn't help believing in happily-ever-after
when handsome amnesiac Blake Hunt landed on her doorstep—
with four-month-old twins. But once regained, would Blake's
memory include a knowledge of the love they'd shared?

#1251 THE BRIDE-IN-LAW—Dixie Browning
His father had eloped! And now Tucker Dennis was faced with
the bride's younger niece, Annie Summers. Annie only wanted
her aunt's happiness, but when she met Tucker, she couldn't help
but wonder if marrying him would make *her* dreams come true.

#1252 A DOCTOR IN HER STOCKING—Elizabeth Bevarly
From Here to Maternity
He had promised to do a good deed before the end of the day,
and Dr. Reed Atchinson had decided that helping pregnant
Mindy Harmon was going to be that good deed. The stubborn
beauty had refused his offer of a home for the holidays—but
would she refuse his heart?

#1253 THE DADDY SEARCH—Shawna Delacorte
Lexi Parker was determined to track down her nephew's father.
But the man her sister said was responsible was rancher
Nick Clayton—a man Lexi fell in love with at first sight. Would
Nick's passion for her disappear once he found out why she was
on his ranch?

#1254 SAIL AWAY—Kathleen Korbel
Piracy on the high seas left Ethan Campbell on the run—and in
the debt of his rescuer, Lilly Kokoa. But once—*if*—they survived,
would Ethan's passion for Lilly endure the test of time?